DEAR TUI, A WARNING

M. C Ronen

mcronenauthor.com

ISBN-13: 979-8-3792-1152-3

To dad

For always asking when the next book is coming

PRAISES FOR 'DEAR TUI, A WARNING'

"The story's narrative allure is irresistible, each page a siren's call, weaving an intricate tapestry that intellectually and emotionally envelops the reader. The narrative's potency is rivaled only by the eloquence of Ronen's prose. Dear Tui, A Warning is a compelling call for self-reflection and taking action. I believe people of all ages can benefit from this book, as its messages are timeless. More than just advice, it offers a look at possible futures, urging us to make changes while we still can. It's definitely worth a read. Rating: 5"
Literary Titan

"This brilliant, gripping, page-turner of a novel is a warning to all of us. It should be mandatory reading. Let's pray its prophecies don't come true."
Jane Velez-Mitchell, New York Times Best-selling Author, UnchainedTV Founder

"DEAR TUI, a warning is an emotional rollercoaster. M.C Ronen perfectly combines grief, despair, and fear, with love, hope and relationship dynamics. It's a gripping read and a rallying cry to make changes now to avoid this dystopian future laid out in the novel."
Peter Egan, Actor and Activist

"This novel is brilliant. It's very dark and paints a realistic sign of what's to come if we continue with business as usual. It is clear Maya has poured her heart and soul into this novel. She is a brilliant writer."
Anita Krajnc, Co-founder and Executive Director of The Save Movement and Campaign Coordinator for Plant Based Treaty

"Great story and could so easily come true, we need the next generation of eco activists more than ever and this book will inspire them."
Dale Vince, Green Industrialist, and Eco Activist

"As a medical doctor who reads far too much science, it is wonderful to immerse myself in some brilliant fiction. However, this engaging story will not be too far off from the hard truth unless we change our current practice and protect the health of the environment, the animals, and ultimately of ourselves."
Dr Ishani Rao, NHS GP and conservation medic, Buckets of Love Founder

"M. C Ronen takes readers on a dark, ominous journey into a dystopian future, and blurs the line between fiction and reality. DEAR TUI, a Warning combines fear and adventure and confronts the reader with the undeniable issues of climate change. The novel seemingly presents us with a choice, continue as we are and face the devastating reality presented within the story, or make real change now to write a new chapter. What would you do?"
Dr Mya-Rose 'Birdgirl' Craig, Author, and Activist

"Dear Tui is a story of resilience, hope, and courage in the face of adversity and loss. It challenges us to be mindful, imagine a different future and take action for a better world as we grow up."
John Paul Jose, Environmental & Climate Justice Advisor and Activist

"DEAR TUI, is a gripping and emotional story, with a wake-up call of what we must save for those we love and the planet we inhabit."
Dominique Palmer, Climate Justice Activist

"A chilling warning on the realities of climate catastrophe and a compelling testament to the resilience of the human spirit, 'Dear Tui' is a must-read for anyone who cares about the future of our planet and the stories we leave behind."
Dr Alan Desmond, Medical Doctor, and Author

"I can't stop thinking about it. I couldn't put it down. The love of a mother for her daughter, a sister for her brother, a wife for a husband woven within the horrors of the landscape they live within, spurred on by human greed and selfishness perfectly balances both the beauty and the destruction humans are capable of. This book and you are true inspiration. Thank you for writing this book."

Kimberly Winters, CPC, ELI-MP, Creator & Host of Did You Bring the Hummus Podcast

ACKNOWLEDGEMENTS & THANKS

There is a famous saying, 'It takes a village to raise a child'. If a book is born out of one's creativity, then similarly, it takes a village to support the author and get the book out into the hands of readers. People's support, encouragement, advice, mentoring, and cheering for you, as an author, isn't to be taken for granted. Such people get involved simply because they believe in you, in your books, and in the message that you're trying to push through. I feel incredibly privileged that my 'village' included the following people to whom I am deeply and forever grateful:

To **Jo Frederiks**, one of my absolute favourite artists, for agreeing to create the stunning cover art for this book before you'd read a single word of it! Such was your trust in me. I am absolutely honoured that your inspirational talent is the beautiful suit my book wears.

To **Emma Hammersley**, for reading the very first draft, and kindly providing me with your sensible suggestions, even while you were drowning in the Auckland floods.

To two phenomenal women - **Jane Velez-Mitchell**, journalist, *New York Times* best-selling author, animal rights activist, environmentalist, and Founder of *UnChainedTV,* and **Anita Krajnc**, Founder and Executive Director of *The Save Movement,* and *Plant Based Treaty.* To those who don't know, these two women are absolute legends in their fields. They never cease speaking up for the planet, emphasising our precarious future here, while rising up against the cruel exploitation and killing of billions of animals, which is not only deeply immoral, but also jeopardises all our future lives on this planet. Thank you so much for believing in my book, endorsing it, and offering me your wise and extremely generous support, opening doors I could only dream about before. Truly, I am standing on the shoulders of giants.

Thank you to the ethically driven PR specialists, **Caroline Burgess-Pike**, and **Hayley Smith**, of Eden Green PR in the UK, for working so hard in your mission to get the book into as many hands as possible. You're both as nice as you're professional, and I'm so glad our paths have crossed.

To **Katrina Fox, Kathleen Gage, Lisa, and David Pannell**, all are business, media, strategic, marketing, public relations gurus, whom I absolutely admire. Thank you for always being so generous with your advice, support, good ideas, and encouragement.

Thank you to all my beloved and supportive friends, with special thanks to **Jackie Norman, and Gareth Scurr** (previously of *Vegan FTA)*, for continuously supporting, promoting, and assisting me in getting my message out. You're two of the loveliest people I know.

To *The Vegan Publisher*, **Mitali Deypurkaystha**, for some of the greatest tips and advice I received in my writing career.

Deep, heartfelt thanks to **The Budget Committee** of The Save Movement/Plant Based Treaty for your incredible and encouraging generosity! I'm blown away by your goodwill. Also – to all the **very kind and lovely people – family, friends, new acquaintances, and complete strangers - who contributed to my crowdfunding**, created to ensure my team can plough through with the book's marketing plan. I am so grateful for every single person who trusted and believed in me and in my mission. I hope this book will indeed inspire the sort of change you were all willing to support. Thank you so much!

Thank you to **the readers**. Thank you to the early reviewers for volunteering to read and provide your reviews and your insights. I truly appreciate that!

To the kind and generous **endorsers of this book**, some of you people I've been admiring from afar for a long time - your kind and encouraging words are simply phenomenal. Thank you so much for taking the precious time out of your busy schedules to spend time with Juniper, Tui, and their collapsing world. I am so very deeply grateful for your support.

Thank you to the vegan community. Thank you to all the incredible, selfless, dedicated, compassionate, animal rights activists worldwide, with a well-deserved, special mention of three of the bravest wāhine (women) activists here in Aotearoa New Zealand, my friends, and my inspirations, all are powerhouses of compassion, determination, and moral integrity: **Elin Arbez, Summer Jayne, and Sandra Kyle**. Thank you.

And of course, last but absolutely not least - thank you to my deeply, deeply beloved family. To my amazing **mum and dad**, thank you for your love and support and for always thinking the world of me. Mum, thank you also for your exceptional, overwhelming generosity. To my rock, my bestie who is my beautiful **husband**; my clever, gorgeous, compassionate, and talented **son and daughter**, who are both the apples of my eye; my two lovable **dog children**, one a crazy extrovert, the other shy and reserved, always at my side, and the best writing buddies one can wish for; and my cute as a button old **rabbit**. You make it all worthwhile.

Cover image: Jo Frederiks - jofrederiksart.com
Images of hourglass: macrovector on Freepik.com

A NOTE FROM THE AUTHOR

Truth must be confessed: I have a rich imagination and vivid fear of what climate change might do to us. Writing, for me, is not only a creative outlet and a form of activism, but also a bit of self-therapy. I write because I'm afraid. The fact that climate change is already actively unleashing extreme weather conditions, such that I so far could only imagine, should fill your heart with dread as well.

I'd written *'DEAR TUI, a Warning'*, over the months of September, October, November, and December 2022. The first draft was finished prior to Christmas 2022. The devastating floods that hit Auckland, Northland and Gisborne, New Zealand, at the end of January 2023, which were quickly followed by the horrendous impact of Tropical Cyclone Gabrielle, in February 2023, had played out almost as if whole chapters in this book were a screenplay for mother nature to enact. This book was not influenced by these events, it predated them.

Please allow yourself to get very scared and please take action.

Thank you,

M. C Ronen

2063

One

We shouldn't be outside on a day like this.

The thought keeps eating at me, as the old car attempts to breach another deep mud swamp. We managed to escape a few mud-pits before, but this one appears to wish to swallow us whole. From my position on the back seat, I can see the worried looks exchanged between Tāne, the driver, and Greta-Jade, his girlfriend, on the passenger seat. Tāne flattens the biofuel pedal, the car's engine roars and whines, the wheels slide this way and that, but we seem to be stuck. Properly stuck, this time. *Shit.*

"I'll jump out and push, you grab the wheel," Tāne says to Greta-Jade.

"Tāne, no!" I burst out, a little louder than intended. The worry and frustration of having been forced to come out on a day like this has built up inside me for a bit too long.

They both look at me with bewilderment and some worry. Perhaps they are a little surprised by the authority in my voice. Perhaps they expected me to be more supportive of any action that could get us out of here.

"It's raining too hard, and the mud is too deep!" I try to explain.

"Juniper," Tāne says, with his deep and calm voice, "if I don't jump out to push, we'll be stuck here for God knows how long. We'll miss the wedding."

The wedding. Trust Tui to plan her wedding in some god-forsaken location she discovered, in the worst part of the Wairepo Domain, in the middle of July. I swear this girl is trying to make sure I die before I'm fifty.

"But…" I try to insist, "your shoes! And your clothes!"

"I have spares," he smiles. "I knew this might happen."

"We can't stay here, it's not safe," Greta-Jade says, some urgency in her voice.

The windows are all foggy, the air inside is musty, and suddenly I find it a little hard to breathe in the car.

"Tāne," I say, my voice pleading.

"I'll be OK, Juniper. It's not that deep," he says, and jumps out before I have time to regroup and protest.

Greta-Jade lifts herself from the passenger seat, half bent she sends her long legs from one side of the car to the other, scootches over and drops herself behind the wheel. I can hear Tāne yelling something from the back. Greta-Jade presses the biofuel pedal. The car heaves, roars, and slides sideways. She lifts her foot. Tāne is still yelling.

I can feel my breaths becoming heavy. *What if he falls back into the mud? What if the car wheels run over him? What if he drowns?* The thought of Tāne drowning in the mud sends waves of cold fright up and down my spine.

Greta-Jade presses the biofuel pedal with the fervour and deliberation of someone who is as terrified as they are determined. The crushing mayhem of the rain hitting us relentlessly from above, the desperate roar of the engine, Tāne's yells at the back, and the mud-fest of deep splatters underneath us, all start to feel like physical assault. I reach with my hands to cover my ears. My vision is blurry. I can hear myself shouting something. I think I'm yelling "Tāne! Tāne!" but it might be "Enav!" I'm not sure. I suspect it's the latter, as suddenly Greta-Jade lifts her foot from the biofuel pedal and turns her head back to look at me, worried.

"Juniper? Are you alright?" she asks.

I'm not sure. I don't know.

"There's an oxygen canister to your left-hand side!" She sounds alarmed. "Juniper!"

I don't want to use the oxygen. Those things cost a small fortune.

"I'm fine, I'm fine," I manage to mumble. In a moment of panic, I reach into my pocket; *are they still there?* My hand can feel the two folded papers. I exhale. *Still there.*

Another thought strikes my heart with deep dread. *Tāne. Where is Tāne?* I can feel the fear so real; its cold fingers clutch my throat. *Where is Tāne? It isn't safe outside!* I want to yell to Greta-Jade, but just then, the driver's door opens. Tāne is there, drenched to the bone, and covered in mud.

"A couple of big pushes, babes," he says. "I put some wood

panels I found under the wheels – it should do it." Without waiting for an answer, he closes the door, and not too long after, his yells can be heard from the back.

Again, the engine roaring, and the rain pounding, and the muffled yelling, and the mud splattering, and Greta-Jade with her aggressive 'C'mon! C'mon!' and my thoughts crawling to the darkest corners, all the way to Enav. I find myself bent forward on my seat, rocking myself back and forth, my arms over my head, big tears rolling down my cheeks. *Dammit Tui, why today? Why here?*

A sudden jolt forward, a sudden roar of the engine, a shriek of triumph, and I knew that we were free. Greta-Jade returned to her seat, Tāne threw himself back behind the wheel.

"Good work, babes," he says to her, smiling.

They don't look back at me. Perhaps they know where my thoughts went, and they just don't want to acknowledge it. Perhaps they feel a little overwhelmed by my reaction. I don't know. We move on.

Two

"Mum! Oh my God, you look like shit! What happened to you?" Tui welcomes me at the hotel, her arms already wrapped firmly around me, her lips pressed against my neck in a big, loud kiss. "But you smell nice!" she says, her smile bright and beautiful. She looks stunning in her second-hand wedding dress, knee-length, figure hugging, off-white lace, and delicate fabric.

Now, this was the thing with Tui; no matter how angry you were, no matter how much you felt like shouting at her, '*What were you thinking?*' you just couldn't stay mad at her for long. Or at all. She was always radiating positivity, always so genuine and so personable, it was disarming.

"You couldn't have had it somewhere else?" I manage to ask her, but with a lot less anger than originally intended.

"Mum! Look at this place!" she twirls me around a bit, to make sure I soak it all in. "Original nineteen eighty-four Bay Springs hotel! Everything is original here, the gardens are a bit boggy, yeah, but still amazing – check out the ceiling. Isn't it marvellous?"

I have to admit it's quite special. Not many original pre-crises buildings were left standing, and none as complete as this hotel. How it survived the violent elements or the looting that followed, I couldn't tell. I suspect some of the 'original' features were a later addition.

The hall where we gather is rectangular and long, with white walls decorated with large mirrors in brass frames. Low-hanging, sad-looking chandeliers dot the pretty, delicately-decorated high ceiling, remnants from days when their richly glittering light had filled this space, but now orphaned and dusty with lack of use. There is no electricity here. Two long tables at the centre of the room are laden with candles. Even though it is barely four in the afternoon, the sky outside, grey, and stormy, is already dark, and the candles are all lit.

"You should have left earlier, I told Tāne!" Tui says, rebuffing my unspoken complaint. "And you should have travelled with Meva's family. Who travels alone, for crissake? Don't you know people still get murdered for biofuel? Or oxygen?" A quick shadow casts over her face, just at the split second when she realises what she's just said, but it's over in a flash.

"I have something for you, Tui," I manage to mumble, my hand absentmindedly sent into my pocket, feeling the folded pieces of paper inside.

"OK. But not now," she replies. "Soon, all right?" and she's off, her arms flying to hug Greta-Jade.

I follow her with my eyes, in awe. Sometimes I can't believe she is my flesh and blood, this beautiful, warm, and lovable bird. Her dark hair is nicely braided and pinned at the back with an elegant hair clip. She reminds me of her father. What wouldn't he have given to be here, with us.

I'm not sure what to do with myself, so I walk to the large window and look outside. How anyone can think this boggy, colourless, stormy mess is 'amazing', I don't know. Only those who were not yet born in The Before could think that. *They don't know how it used to be. They don't know…*

"Juniper!" A radiant blond throws herself at my shoulders.

"Meva!" I blurt, catching my breath, looking at her as she disentangles herself from me. She is a dashing young woman. "You look beautiful."

"Thank you," she smiles, looking at me with a hint of worry. "Would you like to use the bathroom? The soap is divine, locally-made, and there are beautiful, soft towels and a large mirror."

I realise I look even worse than I imagine. I smile and nod. I could do with a few moments on my own.

Inside the large bathroom, merry candles welcome me. The space is a bit musty. A tall and slim oxygen canister is waiting in the corner, at the ready. These things have become a standard everywhere. I watch my reflection in the mirror, with dismay. I have aged. I trace the new webs of wrinkles at the sides of my eyes, the worry ravine that halves my forehead in two. Life has left a mark. I pour some cold water into the basin and wash my face with my hands. The hit of the cold water on my face is refreshing yet stinging and unpleasant. *I can remember warm water. I can remember hot baths.*

I can sense salty tears betraying me, as they start pooling in my eyes. Tears of sorrow, of longing and of anger. I drench my face again, refusing to lose myself in painful memories again. *This is Tui's wedding, pull yourself together.* I exhale long and hard. Out of my handbag

I draw a prickly old hairbrush and try to assume some semblance of a tidy appearance. My unruly short, dark hair has other ideas *'Stop it!'* I say to the woman in the mirror. I wonder if she'd listen.

Three

Tui had asked Tāne, a few weeks earlier, to walk her down the aisle. When she told me, with great delight, I felt like a knife had cut me in half. On one hand, I was sincerely happy. Tāne wasn't Tui's real brother, and her asking him was proof that they grew to share a closeness, the kind that I hoped they'd share, from the day Rāwiri and I introduced them, his son, and my daughter.

On the other hand, I can't lie, I felt more than a bit jealous. I always thought that, since we have no blood relatives left, she'd ask me. I would have been so proud.

Stood up in the front row of several old 'original' chairs, I look back at her and my heart is bursting with pride anyway. Her arm on Tāne's, now changed and cleaned, they look every inch the doting brother and radiant sister. She is so beautiful. I can't avoid reminiscing of all the hardships and challenges life has thrown at us. Curveball after curveball. There were days I wasn't sure we'd survive. But we did, and Tui not only survived, but she thrived.

'This is the one life I've got and I'm gonna live it, Goddamit!'

I remember her, the day her Uncle Enav died. She was flustered and angry at the world, angry at me for losing faith with life on this forsaken planet. She was determined to live, to really live. Her face was red and eyes ablaze. She was only eighteen. She refused to give up. She refused to sink into despair when it had seemed despair was the only thing left. Not for Tui.

I quickly wipe a few persistent tears from the corner of my eye. Tui passes me by and winks at me whimsically, smiling from ear to ear.

At the makeshift altar Meva is waiting, visually shaking with uncontrollable excitement. She reaches her hand out to Tui, who grabs her firmly.

Tāne leaves to stand next to Greta-Jade, across the aisle from me. He is beaming.

The brides face each other. There is no electricity in this place, but there is plenty between those two. You can feel it.

Happiness was possible, after all.

Four

Just one of the two long tables is enough to seat us all. No one is at either head of the table. Tui is to my right, Tāne to my left. Meva's father, who also officiated the beautiful ceremony, is facing me, with his third, or maybe it's his fourth wife, I'm not sure, to his left. Meva's younger brother perished in the Big Famine. I suspect this shared loss is what brought her and Tui together. Tui was only six years old when her father and younger sister died. I doubt very much she remembers either of them, but their loss had affected her deeply. She was always looking for that missing sibling. Maybe that's why she loved Tāne so much, almost from the start.

The thought of the Famine leads me to wonder what will be served for us to eat. Food was still hard to come by. We were fighting for every yield of apples, corn, beans, carrots, and potatoes in our sad little home garden. Double-fenced with high barbed wire, our patch still was often mugged. I can't remember when I last had a fresh loaf of bread.

I can remember the smell of freshly baked, warm bread.

Suddenly, into the room stomps a robust woman with short,

blond hair, dragging behind her a slim blond boy of about nine years, who is protesting vociferously. I recognise them as Meva's aunt and cousin. When the boy was nearly two years old, he fell and hurt his head on the hard floor. After that day, his personality and behaviour changed. He became a little different. It was a widely known fact in the family that he could speak with angels.

"I'm so sorry, I'm so sorry," the woman says, puffed and sweaty. She pulls a chair next to Meva's father, making a great fuss about it all. "Uriah wasn't feeling well just before, so we went up to our room, and we both fell asleep, can you believe it! We've missed the ceremony, haven't we?"

She tsks loudly, clearly displeased with her son, ensuring we all understand this was all the boy's fault. All the time, the boy remains standing, looking at the floor.

"I'm so sorry, Meva, you look beautiful. Tui, you too. I'm really sorry!"

"It's OK," Meva says calmly. "You're on time for the fancy dinner."

"Juniper," she finally acknowledges me, "nice to see you again."

"Nice to see you too, Gwyneth," I say with as much kindness as I can muster. "Hi, Uriah!" I say to the boy.

Ever since Meva had entered our lives, and we got to meet her family, I firmly thought that other than Meva herself, Uriah was the only other likable person of that little tribe. I liked him a lot. I loved his peculiarity. I believed wholeheartedly that the boy could communicate with angels. I also firmly believed that he never fell, but was dropped.

"Juniper!" the boy cries with obvious joy, dislodges himself from his mother's hold and runs to me. He throws himself at me for a hug. I put my arms around him.

He is so thin. I worry for him.

"How have you been doing, young man?" I ask him.

"I saw an armadillo!" the boy says very loudly, nearly shouting.

"An armadillo?" I smile.

"It wasn't an armadillo," his mother shakes her head, looking at us apologetically. "I told you, Uriah, there are no armadillos here, there never were."

"I saw it!" the boy insists.

"I believe you," I whisper in his ear. Not that I did, but I wanted him to feel that there was someone who was clearly on his side.

"Stop encouraging him, Juniper," Meva's father says. "It's not good for him."

"There's no harm in seeing armadillos here and there, Melvin," I say nonchalantly.

"Come take a seat, Uriah," Meva's father calls his nephew, authoritatively. The boy, reluctantly, obeys. He takes a seat next to his mother, facing Meva.

*

My eyes nearly pop out of their sockets when I see four loaves brought to the table, with dip dishes of olive oil.

"How did you manage to get these?" I whisper in disbelief in Tui's ear.

"Oooph, goodness, did you kill someone to get these?" Meva's father is asking.

Meva and Tui giggle.

"That's where most of your kind contribution went to, Dad," Meva says, laughing.

I realise that clearly, Meva's dad helped the brides with this wedding considerably more than I did.

"I wonder where they got the wheat from," Meva's stepmother says. She's a meek woman who always seemed very dull to me. I can't recall ever exchanging more than a few sentences with her.

"Not everywhere is as hopeless as you think," Tui says.

"I actually think it's probably worse than I think," Meva's father says. "Didn't they say oxygen will run out by twenty seventy-two?"

"Stop that, Melvin. Not now," Meva's stepmother castigates him in a lowered voice.

"Dad, you're always such a pessimist!" Meva tells him, sounding quite didactic, as if she were the adult and he was the child. To illustrate her rejection of his claims, she inhales deeply. "There, still alive."

"It's definitely getting worse, and you know it," Meva's dad says. "In fact, I'd be surprised if we even have to twenty seventy-two." He points his finger at his daughter. "And don't think we don't know – all of us here - that it's you two radicals, and your nutty friends, that we have to thank for it!" he says, with some temper.

"Melvin," his wife nudges him.

"Are you referring to Oxy-mask Limited? Those conglomerated abusers and thieves?" Meva asks, with some hard-to-control rising rage. Tui puts her hand on Meva's shoulder, to calm her down.

"You know I am!" Melvin says. "Don't you agree with me, Juniper?" he says and looks at me, anticipatingly.

I don't know quite what to say to that, when—

"How come you married a girl?" Uriah throws his question in the air, very loudly.

"Uriah!" his mother reproaches him.

"It's OK," Meva says, with kindness. "I've already explained it to you Uriah, I love Tui. She's the love of my life. She's my best friend. It doesn't matter that she's a girl. Don't you think?"

"Yes!" Uriah agrees loudly, smiling from ear to ear. "I also love Tui!" he giggles.

The beautiful scent of the warm bread wafts into my nostrils and I salivate so hard I have to drink some water.

Seeing that, and given that no speeches were made yet, Meva's father jumps to his feet. He raises his glass and looks to Tui and Meva.

"Meva. Tui. You are the two most beautiful young ladies I've ever met, and I say that with the utmost objectivity!"

Meva and Tui snigger.

"The love you share is so precious, and more so is your strong friendship and trust of each other," he smiles kindly at his daughter, and mine. "This sort of bond that you have is not to be taken lightly; not in this day and age, not in the sort of society that we turned out to be," he lowers his voice, maybe so that the few people who work at the hotel don't think of him as some hateful radical.

"Dad..." Meva says softly, perhaps anticipating there is worse to come. But her father just smiles and says, with an emotional choke of his voice, "To you both!" and we all raise our glasses and drink our water.

"Maybe you should say a few words," Tāne whispers in my ear. I don't feel comfortable with that. I didn't prepare any speech and I never was very good at speaking off the cuff. Tui hadn't mentioned this would be expected of me today. But Tāne looks at me adamantly, and I feel there is a general expectation around the table, so slowly, I lift myself up and raise my glass.

"Tui, Meva," I smile, thinking quickly of what to say next. "I'm here not only for myself but also, I'm here for Tui's father, Crispin, and her sister, Moana, God rest their souls." Always good to bring the dead to support you, I think. "You look so much like him, Tui."

Tui smiles at me, a gentle smile.

"I know I didn't tell you a whole lot about Crispin and Moana over the years. I never wanted to burden you with stories of that tragedy. To scare you..." I sneak a quick look at Meva's father. He obviously had no issue with doing that. "Truth is, that life wasn't easy for us. We struggled. Meeting Rāwiri and his son, Tāne," I say as I place my hand on Tāne's shoulder, "was one of the only blessings we had known in so many years." I take a deep breath. I wasn't planning for this to get so morbid. "Until you met Meva."

Finally, everyone smiles with some relief. It's a hopeful speech after all.

"You are both so beautiful, so clever, so kind. You're wonderful," I look at Tui intently. I hope she knows how much I love her. "I don't know how you turned out so lovely. I guess I wasn't such a terrible mother after all..." I chuckle, and Tui laughs. "I'm so glad you found each other. Your happiness makes me happy. And I know it makes Crispin happy!"

"And my dad too!" Tāne adds promptly, his glass raised.

"And Rāwiri, of course," I say quickly, as my hand automatically reaches inside my pocket, my breath held, to seek the two folded papers inside. My two sole treasures. With my thumb I make sure both are there. My fingers rest on the thicker of the two. *Rāwiri's poem.* My mind at ease, I exhale softly.

"Heaven is full of my mum's dead lovers," Tui says jokingly, and everyone laughs. I do too. *I can remember, being loved.*

We raise our glasses and drink.

I sit back down. Tui takes my hand and squeezes it with warmth. I kiss her cheek. She's still my little girl. I'd always loved her so much. I expected her, years before she came.

And now, finally, it's time to eat.

Five

We break the bread and dip it in the olive oil. I feel an uncontrollable urge to close my eyes as I savour the homely flavours, treasure the slight saltiness, the touch of sweetness, the hint of sourness. The textures of the soft dough and the crunchy crust. The warmth of the bread with the slight cool of the oil. I used to take these flavours for granted, and now, my mouth is exploding with delight. My memory sends me to Rāwiri, and the flatbread he made at our last Christmas together, and my eyes cloud with tears. I think I might cry.

A young, clean-shaven hotel person, dressed in a dark suit and white shirt, approaches us, pulling a trolly behind him with a large pot of vegetable soup steaming on top of it. He circles around the table, filling small clay bowls and serving us each in turn. I take a spoonful of the rich broth and blow it gently; the steam mists my face.

Another plate is brought to the table, loaded with thinly sliced apples and pears.

"Wow, this is such a beautiful meal!" Greta-Jade is obviously impressed.

"Spare no expense," Meva's father says a little too pompously, and

I think there is a small criticism there directed at me, for not forking out my equal share.

"Thank you, Dad," Tui says, and I can't help but choke on the soup. Why would she call him Dad? He isn't her dad. He's Meva's dad. It was a bit too foreign for me to take.

Tui pats my back as I cough, until I manage to regain my composure. The moment is slightly tense. I doubt she'll call him that, next to me, any time soon.

Melvin doesn't seem to mind. "I remember when they said we should be eating cockroaches and crickets," he mutters. "That could have been a great solution to our current predicament," he slurps his soup loudly.

"Great, eat more animals, that was your solution?" Meva blurts at him. "Trust your generation to *completely* miss the point!"

"Armadillo!" Uriah shouts eagerly.

"Calm down, I never said that." Meva's dad replies to his daughter. "Crickets and cockroaches aren't animals."

"Uh, what are they, then?" she asks, her voice raised.

"I don't know," he isn't fussed. "Disgusting?"

"Every creature has the right to live the life they have! It's all they have! Look what that human-supremacist approach did to the animals, did to the planet... did to all of us!" Meva says, clearly flustered.

I can remember animals.

"Calm down, my love," Tui takes Meva's hand in her hand.

Me and Tui, we never ate animals, or any animal derivatives, ever. My mum was adamant it was morally wrong, so I was brought up like that. But back then, we were the minority. Tui, though, she was born after The Before, when everything was already changing. The only way to save something of life on the planet, they said, was to be completely plant-sufficient. Being vegan was the only solution. If people changed quickly, and fully, life could be saved. But people preferred to change every other small bit and bob, except for their eating pleasures. By the time everything was falling apart, short-sighted political muppets were trying desperately to hard-steer the economy away from animal agriculture. But it was too late. Everything that was done, was done too late.

"Our neighbours down the lane, they have a dog," Meva's dad clearly wasn't done. "An old fella. Very cute. I don't know how they manage to keep him safe."

I can remember dogs. I can remember Johnny.

"Dad!" Meva is clearly growing upset.

"Melvin!" his wife is none too pleased either.

"Armadillo!"

"Uriah!"

I pick a slice of pear and take a small bite. It is ripe and sweet, but I can taste the salty tears at the back of my throat. Memories do that to me, sometimes.

"Tui," I finally manage to get her attention. "I want to give you something." I reach into my pocket and take out the thinner of the two folded papers inside.

She smiles, there is whimsical light in her eyes. I know her curiosity is piqued.

"Is this an old will?" she giggles.

I smile. Not quite. "You know I have nothing to give," I say. "No, this is something else."

I hand her the folded paper. The entire table is focused on it now.

"What is it?" Uriah shouts. "Read it loud!"

With delicate fingers, Tui opens the folds. The whiteness of old is now a deep shade of yellow and stained in parts. This paper, it had seen the climate changing, houses flooded, storms destroy entire communities; it had seen people being murdered, death, violence; it had seen love.

Finally open, she reads it, then turns to me, visibly moved yet confused.

"I wrote it to you when I was nine years old," I said.

"Nine?" she repeats after me, even more confused.

"Yes," I confirm, "and I saved it for you. I saved it all this time."

She smiles.

"Is this the letter you left me on a tree for?" she asks. There's a faint whimsical tone in in her voice.

I shudder. *She remembers! All these years, and she remembers!* I can do nothing but swallow hard and nod slowly.

"It wasn't for long," I whisper finally. I suddenly remember quite vividly the panic that gripped me all those years ago, when I couldn't find the tree on which she was left.

"It's OK, Mum," she says softly and smiles warmly. "I forgave you a long time ago."

I look deep into her eyes. I think she now grasps the deep sentimental and spiritual value this piece of paper holds for me.

"Thank you, Mum," she says with a nod, as she folds it gently and places it inside her own pocket. "It's quite amazing, when you come to think of it," she says, her voice soft. "That you'd written it, and that you saved it all these years."

I smile, tears prick my eyes.

"What did it say?" Uriah shouts to Tui.

"I'll tell you when *you* get married!" she chuckles, and he responds with a laugh.

Now with the note delivered, I feel lighter, sort of weightless. No more do I need to take care of it, to make sure it's still there, to keep it, to worry about it. It feels so joyous, and suddenly—a little sad. The one thing that was with me throughout the years, often on my person, with everything I endured over time—and God knows, there was plenty! —Is finally gone from me.

*

Two hotel people appear, one carries a fiddle, the other an accordion. They start playing a merry little tune. The atmosphere instantly uplifts.

"Let's dance, my love," Tui says to Meva, and the two leave the table. They settle for a small, clear space near the entrance. I watch them dance together, so in love, so happy with each other. A sense of serenity washes over me.

In a funny circumstantial change of roles, it is Uriah who bolts from his seat to the dance floor, with his mother dragging her feet reluctantly behind him. The boy rocks his body with so much joy, his entire being is consumed with the music.

Tāne and Greta-Jade join them on the makeshift dance floor. I keep my head turned to watch them all. I don't feel like making small talk with Meva's father, or his wife. I wish my friend Julianna were here. Tui should have invited her. I asked her to, but they decided to make it 'family only'. Julianna was as close as family to me. But Tui didn't know half of it.

I start feeling a little tired. I wonder when it might be a good time to ask Tui to take me to my room. I have a sense the dancing might last a while, so I lean my head on my arm and close my eyes.

That's why I don't notice her come in.

Six

The commotion on the dance floor jolts me awake. The musicians have disappeared. There's screaming and yelling, but mostly, above all else, there is Uriah's voice, steadily wailing in a strange, loud monotone sound.

She is quite scruffy, drenched, and muddied, looks rugged. Her face, menacing, could use a wash. I can smell her from where I sit. From behind the boy, her left hand is reaching over his left shoulder, holding him tight across the chest. Her right, over Uriah's right shoulder, is holding a massive knife to his neck. This is no play knife. I've seen the likes of it before. People who wield such a knife mean business. It's a weapon and it means to kill. The blade is very sharp; it is poking only very lightly into the boy's skin, and already there is blood. I can tell, instantly, looking into her dull eyes, that the woman is somehow drugged.

I jump to my feet. *How did she get here?* This place is practically in the middle of nowhere. I look around with urgency, assessing Tui's distance from the woman. She seems to be far enough from immediate danger; so are Meva, Tāne and Greta-Jade.

I look for Meva's dad. If anyone amongst us has the ability to deal

36

with something like that, surely, it has to be him. I bet he travels with a small armoury of his own. He is standing by the table, looking intent on action, but immobilised by the clear, immediate danger to his nephew's life.

"No one moves, or I kill him!" the woman yells.

"Don't you dare kill him! Let him go! Let him go, NOW!" the boy's mother screams, utterly hysterical.

I can tell this isn't going to help.

"Please," I say with the calmest voice I can possibly produce under the circumstances, "what do you want?"

Foolishly, I take the tiniest step forward.

"Don't move! I'll kill him! This is your last warning!" she yells.

Uriah's monotonous wailing is disturbing her.

"Shut up! Shut up! I'll cut you up! Shut up!" the woman orders him, highly agitated.

I raise my hands in surrender. "Please, he's got health issues. He's not like any other boy, he can't control himself," I say calmly. I need her to trust me. "Please, don't hurt him."

The woman looks at me, very intently. On some obscure, unspoken level, I feel like there is a sudden, faint connection, somehow. I hope I'm not fooling myself.

"Please, let us know what you want, we might be able to help you."

Uriah's mother is heaving with deep, hysterical inhales. Tui and

Meva are hugging in fright. Tāne is sheltering Greta-Jade behind him. I try to maintain the woman's eyes on me. "Is it food? Would you like our food? We have some to share." I indicate with my head towards the table, where there are enough leftovers for a hungry person to feast on. "I'm sure there's more in the kitchen."

The woman looks at the food. I can see she is salivating. "No!" she finally says. Now I'm surprised. What can she possibly want from us?

"I need oxygen!" she blurts.

"OK. Oxygen." I'm a little relieved. There are a few canisters in the hotel. Surely, we can get her one and avoid bloodshed.

"There's oxygen here!" Meva's father says hurriedly. The woman's fixed attention on me breaks. "I can bring you a canister!" he suggests and is about to turn away from the table.

"Don't move!" she shouts. The knife penetrates into Uriah's neck just a smidgen deeper. He screams wildly. The trickle of blood is morphed into a small and narrow stream. Uriah's shirt starts to soak dark red.

"Wait! Please!" I say urgently, my hands still in the surrender position, my voice as low and as controlled as allowed by the fragile nerves I try so desperately to marshal. "I can take you there. No tricks. Leave the boy, take me. I'll lead you to the bathroom—there is a canister there, I saw it with my own eyes."

The woman stares at me long and hard. "Where is the bathroom?" she finally asks.

"Just over there, to the left, at the end of that small hallway." I indicate with my head. "There's nothing to it, it's really close. Take me—with the knife! I'll show you. Just… leave the boy."

She looks behind her towards the hallway, hesitating.

"Please," I beg her. "I won't run, take me."

"Mum!" I can hear Tui's faint cry of despair from the corner. I don't look at her.

The woman nods. "OK. Show me your pockets, first."

Relieved but wild with fear, I show her my pockets. To my dismay, Rāwiri's poem falls out. "It's just a piece of paper. See, nothing else there," I say.

"Lift your shirt up and turn around in a circle," she orders next.

Slightly embarrassed, I lift my blouse and turn around in a circle. What she could possibly expect me to be hiding under there, I'm not sure.

"OK. Slowly walk to me," she orders.

I take small and slow steps toward her. My knees are buckling, my head spinning. Inside I'm melting with fear, but I manage to keep my outward composure intact.

I'm almost at her side when she shouts to me, "When you're one step from me, turn around with your back to the knife. You'd better do it, or I'll slit his throat AND stick you, hear me?"

"Yes, yes!" I assure her.

Two more tiny steps and I'm there. I turn around. My hands still raised in surrender.

In a single aggressive move, she tosses Uriah away to the left. He drops to the floor, howling. His mother and Tāne quickly crouch down and pull him away from his assailant.

The woman puts the knife to my back. I can feel a burning sting where its sharp pointy end meets my flesh, through the cloth of my blouse.

"Show me!" the woman orders. "Small steps!"

"Mum!" Tui weeps.

"No one dare move when we walk, or I kill her, d'you hear?"

There are whimpers and cries all around. I turn very slowly and start marching, in small and measured steps, towards the hallway. It occurs to me that I don't even know if the canister is full, or how heavy it is. Would she be able to pick it up by herself? Would she ask me to do it and take me away with her? Would she kill me anyway? Step by step we enter the hallway, the party room disappears behind us, with Tui out of my reach, and Rāwiri's poem on the floor.

Seven

The narrow hallway, clad with deep orange wallpaper and lit with thick, white candles, held onto the wall, feels instantly claustrophobic.

"It's behind that door in front of us," I say through clutched jaws, suddenly completely consumed by blind terror. My mouth is dry, cold sweat drips down my spine, and my hands are shaking uncontrollably. In just a few more small steps, I'd be able to reach out my hand in front of me and push the bathroom door open.

We're almost there when the woman yells, "OK, stop! I need to plan this, what's gonna happen inside the bathroom."

Did she just say 'stop'? It takes me completely by surprise and confuses me so much, I take one more automatic step forward, while she stays in her place.

There is a sudden gap between my back and the knife.

"I'm sorry!" I say, and instantly stop, cowering somewhat in fear of her reaction, just at the exact same time as she barks at me again, "I said sto—"

In that very instant, from behind us, at the party room entrance to the hallway, a booming voice is rolling louder than both of us,

"Juniper, move!"

Meva's father got his gun. I knew he had one, it was inevitable. He fires a shot that makes the walls around us shatter and splits my eardrums. I duck. At least, I think I duck. I definitely bend, somewhat. I shriek. Everything happens so quickly. The woman behind me doesn't quite manage to complete the word 'stop', and it's a split of a split of a second before I work out what's happening. I can tell the bullet got her. There is an explosion of blood, and she collapses forward. Her body falls on top of me, topples me over, and we both crash to the floor, through the open bathroom door. I'm not sure if I'm alive or if I'm dead.

Eight

Total mayhem ensues. Someone picks the woman's lifeless body from the top of me and drags her out of there. Half her head is gone. Tui is standing over me. "Mum!" she cries, "are you OK?"

She tries to lift me up, but all she can manage is to sit me a little upwards, leaning against the bathroom wall. I look ahead, and there is the oxygen canister. Prized treasure, still in its place. "Mum, oh my God, you were so brave!" Tui is gushing, deeply emotional.

Tāne, face ashen, is also standing on top of me now. "Are you OK, Juniper?"

I feel very dizzy, my thoughts are spinning. I can't really say if I'm OK. I'm not sure.

"Can you stand up?" Tāne asks me.

I try to lift myself, or maybe just an arm to start with, but everything is very heavy. "I think I need to stay down here for a while," I manage to say, my voice sounding weak and far away.

"Tāne, something's wrong," Tui says hurriedly. "Help me check her." She holds my right arm, he holds the left and they both pull me gently away from the wall and inspect my neck, shoulders, and my back. It's Tui who screams first.

"Mum! Mum!" she cries, in big, heavy sobs. "Help!" she yells out into the hallway, "Help! Help us!"

"I'll get a hotel person to call a doctor," Tāne says as he leaps to his feet.

What doctor does he think he'd get, in this place, blimmin' middle of nowhere… I laugh to myself.

Meva, her father, and Uriah are all now crammed on top of me.

"The knife…" Tui tries to speak but her words fade into a wave of weeps and bawls.

"The woman fell on her with the knife still drawn," Meva's father surmises. I still don't think he's sorry for taking that shot. "Must've pierced her on the way down."

I'm starting to feel very cold.

"Juniper, when you're an angel I'll come and talk to you!" Uriah's shouting to me over Tui's head.

"Oh, I don't think people like me become angels, Uriah," I manage to mumble.

I can still remember… the man in the mud. I can remember… the baby.

"Mum! Hold on! Hold on!" Tui wails, Meva's comforting arms around her.

With the remnants of my fading strength, I reach with my hand into my pocket, trying to feel the other piece of paper still there. Rāwiri's poem. Oh, it's on the floor, in the party room.

"The poem, I dropped it," I manage to say.

"I'll get it," Meva says and disappears.

She returns with Rāwiri's poem and hands it to me. I smile. Everything is fine. Not that I needed the paper, it was only precious because he wrote it, but I knew his words by heart. How did it go… How did it go? Suddenly I panic. I can't remember how it starts, I can only recall a single line, *Here or not, our love will onwards shine…*

"Tāne, we need to lift her up, let's take her to the table," Meva's father says.

Within seconds, Tāne grabs me from the back, Meva's father grabs my legs. They lift me up and take me away. I feel heavy and getting increasingly heavier. My head is spinning. So foggy. *Here or not, our love will onwards shine.* They lay me on the table and lift my soaked blouse. I'm not sure where I am anymore. People all around me are shouting, crying, it's such a cacophony of blurring sounds, the room spins. *Here or not, our love will onwards shine.* I'm very tired. I'm so tired. Wait, is it Johnny? I think I can hear Johnny. Maybe. I just want… I just want to sleep. Just for a second. I'll be up in a moment. Just, let me sleep. The world disappears into darkness. My ears can no longer decipher the muffled sounds, there are no more words, only a distant hum, fading further and further away; only one thing I can hear quite clearly still.

"Hi, Juniper."

Uriah.

FIVE

YEARS

EARLIER:

2058

Nine

My feet are killing me. The sole of my right shoe is torn in places from the outsole and toe cap, and now the shoe is filled with mud, and I can't walk properly. I'm not sure where I could get another pair. I don't think I could afford a new pair. I may need to ask Julianna. I reckon we're the same shoe size.

I can see Julianna is already waiting for me at the old bus stop. She is waving. I wave back.

I'm a few feet away when she shouts at me, "What happened to your feet?"

I pretend I can't understand what she's saying through her personal Oxy-mask. I don't feel like shouting back at her either.

"Why are you walking funny?" she asks me again when I'm finally near enough.

"I ripped my shoe," I tell her.

"Oh, crap!"

"Do you have any idea where I can get a new pair?" I decide to first ask in a general way, before I start asking for favours.

"Don't you have any other shoes?" she asks.

I shake my head.

"Oh, dear. That's no good. What size are you?"

"Eight, eight and a half."

She nods. "Yeah, you're the same size as me. I'll bring you a pair of mine, tomorrow."

"Are you sure?" Suddenly I feel embarrassed about being such a beggar. I feel so bad about using someone else's shoes. Her shoes. What if she'll need them the day after tomorrow?

"Oh yeah, no worries. I have more than one extra pair," she says, as we start making our way to the entrance.

I keep forgetting that Julianna used to be a very wealthy woman in The Before. She is still so much better off than me, but she doesn't show it, and she certainly doesn't feel like it.

"Thank you, Julianna," I say.

"Don't mention it," she replies, sincerely. "Didn't we agree to take the earlier bus today?" she asks me.

I knew she'd ask. Shall I tell her about the nightmares I still have every night? How I sometimes struggle through the smallest hours just to breathe? How in my dreams I barely escape death by a crazed assassin motivated by hunger; I manage to save myself and Tui by the narrowest of margins… and sometimes I fail? Again and again, I re-live those moments, again and again I wake up disturbed, tired, disoriented.

"Oh, so sorry about that, yes. Tāne and Greta-Jade were staying with me on the weekend, I forgot," I manage to say, eventually. Half of it is true, Tāne and Greta-Jade really did stay the weekend.

"How are they?"

"They're alright. It's always so nice to see them."

"I bet," she says, then more carefully, "Are they still planning to wed?"

I sigh. "I don't know, to be honest. We haven't talked about it."

It's been three years since Tāne brought Greta-Jade home, to introduce us. He'd never brought a girl home before, not since Rāwiri and I were together anyway, so I knew this one was special to him. Rāwiri had passed away a year before, and for Tāne I was the closest thing to a parent that he had left. I remember the night he brought her to dinner like it was yesterday. He was beaming with excitement and so radiating with love. She was a pretty, young woman, with hazel eyes and light brown, wavey hair. 'Coquettish' we would have said in another era, I believe.

"Hi," she shook my hand. "I'm Greta-Jade."

Oh, one of those hyphenated names, I couldn't avoid thinking.

As if reading my mind, she added quickly, "My parents couldn't decide. Dad wanted Jade, Mum wanted Greta, you know, after the famous Greta."

I smiled. There was such an influx of Gretas since the mid-twenty twenties.

"I swear, every day the bus is dropping us further and further away," Julianna mutters under her Oxy-mask.

"Well, it's becoming boggier and boggier, I don't think there's much they can do about it," I say.

"There's much that they can do, they just don't give a shit," she replies.

"I suppose. But work here won't last for much longer. I reckon we'd be finished within six months."

She nods. "What would you do then?"

I shake my head. "I don't know."

I really don't.

We enter the main building, right at the entrance of the dam deconstruction site. As soon as we are inside, we take off our Oxy-masks. There is no need for them; the building is pumped with oxygen around the clock. The building is built of dark, grey stones, sitting low on the ground, its inside oval and cave-like.

Julianna and I work in the office, helping with filings and maintaining financial records. Wages are decent, better than those of the deconstruction workers, outside at every hour of the day, in every sort of weather. The dam—completed and christened only ten years earlier—is being taken down. Built as another quick superglue solution by panic-stricken officials, it was meant to somehow control, and avert, the effects of the world coming to an end. What they didn't expect—even though it was plain to see coming—was for the torrential rains to intensify and spread, for cyclones to constantly arrive at our shores, and for the dam's horrid impact to completely outdo any potential benefit. On its first year it already overflowed, flooding whatever was left of the villages below, those that weren't already wiped out by the rising sea levels. Diverting the excess water to the emergency gorge was futile, as the gorge was also overflowing. This entire area, miles, and miles of it, used to be an incredible conservation area once. A protected, managed, natural park, with native bushland, indigenous wildlife, and unique birds; a thing of real beauty and ecological value. Now, Wairepo Swamp it's called. Everything is destroyed.

Ten

Julianna and I take our lunch break together, always at the same time, sitting at the same place, a small niche in the northern wall. We each take out our soup cans and pour some of the vegetable broths into the cups. We spend a few moments blowing the steam, and then sit quietly sipping the soup. I look around with some sadness. This place is so formidable, it's almost unthinkable that it will soon be shut down.

Julianna nudges me suddenly with her elbow, causing me to spill some of my soup. "That fellow, Declan, is watching you again," she says quietly.

I'm busy wiping my pants, vocally protesting the interruption to my lunch. "How do you know he's looking at me? Maybe he's looking at you?" *We're too old to be having such schoolgirl talk.*

"Nope," Julianna insists, "definitely you."

"He's too young for me," I say.

"Maybe he is, but he's looking. He's definitely interested in you, girl."

I raise my eyes from my cup as I sip. I can see Julianna is right, and he is definitely watching me. I've noticed him noticing me before. He is cute, I admit. But I'm not interested.

"You know, at some point, you'll need to move on from Rāwiri," Julianna says softly.

I know she means well, but I can't.

"He's been dead for what, three years now?" she continues.

"Four," I correct her.

"Well… that's nearly the length of time you'd been with him, isn't it?"

I nod, slowly, but it's not the kind of conversation I'm ready to have. Not even with Julianna who is my best friend. I can't explain to her what Rāwiri meant to me. How he came into my life at a time when every single day I wished it away. The only reason for me to live, the only thing that kept me holding on, was Tui. Meeting Rāwiri was the lifeline I needed. He was the rock I yearned to find. He was older than me, wiser, and he had Tāne, an instant older brother for Tui. Rāwiri saved me. Now, without him, I'm adrift again. But unlike then, Tui is now nineteen and isn't dependent on me as she was before. For me, once more, every day is a struggle. This guy, Declan, he might be cute, and he's quite possibly interested, but he's too young, and I have no energy left to start over with someone.

"I'm just saying," Julianna adds, but isn't saying anything.

We sit quietly for a while longer. It's almost time to get back into the office.

"What about you?" I ask her. "Still with that ex-military dude?"

Julianna giggles. I know she wanted me to ask. She loves talking about him. Some buff, muscly fella she picked up from I can't remember where.

"Best sex I ever had in my life," she chuckles.

I join her chuckles.

"Trust me," she says knowingly, as she covers her soup can and returns it to her backpack, "it seems like all that was missing in my life was a good fuck."

Just as we come to leave, the place begins to shake. Gently at first, then profusely. The ground, the walls, the few tables, and the chairs, everything rocks and rolls. Julianna and I cower, leaning against the wall. There isn't much to hold onto. It takes good few seconds for the shaking to cease.

"I've had it up to here with these earthquakes," Julianna mutters. "How soon before we're all buried alive in here, do you reckon?"

I'd rather not think about it. I worry about Tui and Tāne and Greta-Jade. I hope they're safe. I'm trying to remember where Tui said she'd be. Where Tāne said they were going. I suddenly have an uncontrollable urge to take my stuff and go home.

As if answering my wishes, only moments later, the sound of the emergency alarm rattles the office and the halls.

"Evac!" the dayshift manager puts his head through the door and shouts at no one specifically.

We take our bags, put our Oxy-masks on, and try to be as orderly and casual as we can, leaving the building and congregating outside by the entrance. I pray that we don't need to go back in. *Please, let us go home.* It takes several minutes for the dayshift manager to finally come outside and address us.

"There's been a landslip, folks," he says. "Due to the mud."

"How bad?" someone asks.

"Massive, I'm afraid."

A low hum of worried murmurs ensues.

"I'm afraid I can't let you back in," the dayshift manager says.

Many of the employees are angry about that. They get paid by the hour, and now they have less to bring home. I feel for them. I can relate to their worry. But my heart rejoices for the early discharge.

Julianna and I break out from the crowd and start making our way to the new makeshift bus stop, a mile and a half away. Just as we start walking, the rain begins falling again, angry, and heavy. I wobble on my broken shoe, sliding inside it with all the mud. I can feel a blister forming.

"Remember when rain used to drizzle?" I ask Julianna.

"And mudslides were something we did at the waterpark," she adds.

We reach the old bus stop, where the drop-offs and pick-ups used to be. Now the bus can't get here.

"Remember how we used to complain the bus stop was too far from the entrance?" I mutter.

"Yeah, a lot of the things we used to complain about would be luxury today," she agrees.

As we pass the old, falling-apart stop I see some invisible hands have covered the old station with Climate Revenge posters. I'd found a few similar posters in Tui's room a few months ago. I wonder if my daughter has turned into an anarchist. My mum would've been so proud.

Instinctively, I take my Oxy-mask off.

"You're brave," Julianna says.

"We've been told we had to wear Oxy-masks from the moment we arrive at the bus-stop, or as soon as we depart from it. Well, we just departed. That was the stop."

Julianna looks back. There are small groups of employees walking further away, behind us.

"What if someone tells on you?" she sounds genuinely concerned.

"What's to tell? That, there, was the bus stop. I don't have to wear the mask from that point. I hate these masks. They're uncomfortable and they're addictive. Honestly, look—there is still oxygen in the air, we don't have to wear it. The only reason they force us to, is because the people who own the dam also own the oxy factory. Clearly, Julianna."

She hesitates, then takes hers off as well.

"I can't stand these masks either."

Eleven

I get off the bus two stops after Julianna's. It takes more than an hour for the driver to manoeuvre around mudslides, landslips, sinkholes, and newly-formed mini-swamps. Even still, there is about ten minutes of fast walking in the wet and foggy weather left for me, before I reach the neighbourhood. With my shoe being in the state that it's in, it takes me twenty.

In The Before, areas of congregated living like these would not even be considered neighbourhoods. Simple shacks, made of wood and corrugated iron. Refuge for those who were forced to move too often and were left with nothing.

I can't bear to think about being forced to evacuate this house of mine, again. I am tired of moving. Of seeking shelter.

My childhood house was claimed by the rising sea water. The first house I shared with Crispin was flooded countless times, until it remained permanently flooded. Before I moved in with Rāwiri, I lived in a house that was destroyed by a massive tornado, while elsewhere, my brother's house was hit by a severe storm, possibly the first category-five cyclone ever to hit our shores. Seeking to keep out of the reach of rising rivers and seawater, Rāwiri and I moved to this house I still currently live in, midway up a hill. Mudslides and landslips, however, have already claimed a decent chunk of the houses up the road. Mother Earth was really trying her best to spit us humans out. I guess it's only a matter of time before my house disappears into the insatiable thick, brown, pasty water below, like the rest of them. I just hope Tui has already left home when that happens.

It's already quite dark in the neighbourhood when I arrive, drenched by rain and half-covered in mud. Modest as the house was, I was looking forward to a simple meal, a book I borrowed long since from Julianna, and a comfortable bed. The door isn't locked; there is nothing to steal.

"Tui?" I call into the silent darkness. No one answers. She's still out, wherever 'out' is. She is quite politically-motivated, my Tui, engaged in plenty of climate emergency grassroots groups. Unlike my generation when we were in our teens, back in the age of wealth and prosperity in The Before. We were so sombre and depressed, goth and emo, sceptical of any form of liveable future, when we still had it all. This generation of young people, who were actually losing everything at an alarming speed, were surprisingly hopeful.

I take off my drenched raincoat and waterproof over-pants and hang them to dry, then walk around the small space and light some candles.

Next, I go to the small washroom at the back, take the small copper tub and fill it with a little cold water. I place a small cube of soap in the water. As I pick up the washing cloth, I decide to add some boiled water to the mix. It's not a luxury I practiced very often, but as I was home earlier than usual, I didn't mind waiting for the water to boil. I could even throw a few potatoes to the same pot of boiled water, after I spooned a couple of cups out and into the bath.

I come out of the washroom into the main room and my heart nearly pops out of my mouth from the shock.

"Hi!" he says, smiling.

I can't control the scream that blurts out of me.

"What are you doing in my house?" I say. My voice shakes as I try to catch my breath.

"The door was open, I thought it was an invitation."

The door is always open. "Were you following me?"

He chuckles. "Like you didn't notice?"

"I didn't. I didn't notice," I say firmly. *What does he want? When is Tui home?*

"Oh, c'mon," he says, still smiling, as he takes a few steps towards me. I take a few steps back. "You're always playing hard to get, Juniper."

"I'm not playing anything," I say in a rush, trying to go in my head over all the possible encounters we'd ever had at work, when I might have—unintentionally—given him a signal, small as it possibly was, that I was interested. I'm sure there were none.

He's now very close to me. Towering over me. He reaches with his right hand and strokes my long, wet hair, down my cheek, down over my breast. He's lingering on my breast. I hold my breath.

"Declan," I say, trying to sound composed, "you're much too

young for me, don't you think?"

"Nonsense," he says. "How old are you?"

I'm not going to answer that.

"You're definitely much younger than me," I mumble. His hand still on my breast, squeezing it slightly.

"Are you a hot old lady, then?" he asks, laughing. "I don't mind that one bit. Always wanted my own MILF."

He puts his left hand on my chin and turns my face to face him, catching my eyes in his. I can't believe I thought he was cute, even good-looking, before. He utterly terrifies me.

I always feared something like this could happen, living in such an unlockable house. After Rāwiri's death I used to put a chair against the door-handle every single night. But time passed, no one other than myself, Tui, Tāne and Greta-Jade ever came even close to this place, so I grew complacent.

"You turn me on," he says, and leans closer. His mouth is pressing against my mouth. I'm revolted.

"No!" I shout and push him away. "I'm not interested!"

I try to run to the door but he's quicker than me and blocks the way out.

"Then why were you leading me on? Why did you lead me to your house?" he says, now sounding angry.

"I didn't lead you! I was just going home!" I shout. "I'm not looking for a relationship! I'm not interested!"

He isn't smiling. "You're just a tease," he says, and walks towards me.

"No!" I scream, then "Help! Help me!" knowing well enough that no one will come. People lost all traces of solidarity a long time ago. The rush of rainwater on the corrugated iron drowns my screams anyway.

He grabs me firmly and tries to push me on the table, but I stumble and fall to the ground, hitting my head as I meet the floor. It's instantly pounding from the hit, but I still manage to turn over, and try to crawl away. It's only a matter of seconds before he's lying on top of me, on the floor. He flips me over, and pins me down, my back to the floor, facing him.

My legs are kicking so hard, still, he manages to strip me of my pants and undies, chuckling as he does. I'm horrified to think he believes this is some kind of foreplay.

I struggle, try to wiggle away from his hold, but he's so much stronger, and so determined. In my head, I know, there's no way he'll be leaving this house without doing what he came for. But I wonder if killing me is also in the plan.

The more I try to push him away, the rougher he gets. I don't want to feel him, I don't want to know what's happening. I can feel his hands in my hair, holding me as if we were lovers. I try to detach myself from here, disconnect from my body, send my mind elsewhere. My tears are choking me. I weep uncontrollably. I can smell his breath; I can hear his pleasure moans. I feel sick. I want to die.

No, I don't want to die. I don't. There's Tui. I need to live.

Twelve

He's finished. I can tell he's just climaxed.

"Baby," he says, "that was awesome."

I feel so much pain, shame, and rage. Through a thick veil of tears, I can see he's smiling. His hand is in my hair again, still playing the fake lover. He seems to finally be ready to roll off me when he curls himself backwards and makes a sudden choking sound. I don't want to look. I don't want to know what has just happened to me.

But the choking sounds don't stop. He's definitely choking.

"Help me!"

Did he just say, 'Help me'?

"Help me, Juniper!"

It's Julianna!

From however far away I've been, I come back instantly. I slide away from underneath Declan to see him being choked from behind by Julianna. She's holding a string to his neck and pulling it tight. He's giving quite a fight, but she's holding on.

"Smash his head, or something!" she yells, puffed from the effort.

I leap to my feet, grab the first pot I can find, and rush back. I stand on top of him. I can see his eyes are frantically rushing around, seeking mine, pleading. I smash the pot hard on his face. There is the sound of cracking bones. Julianna is still pulling hard on the string. I smash his face one more time. Declan goes still and limp.

We stand quietly for a while, facing each other, panting. I grab my pants and undies from the floor and put them on. The rain still falls outside. No one heard a thing.

I want to cry, but there's nothing there. Julianna rubs her palms against each other. They're red and slightly bleeding, from the effort. She opens her hand and down drops a black shoestring.

"I decided to come by and bring you the shoes tonight, so you don't limp your way to work tomorrow."

I fall on her shoulders. I want to say 'thank you' but instead, I only heave with anxiety and shock.

She hugs me tightly. "You'll be OK," she says into my ear, "hear me? You'll be OK!"

I nod.

"Let me get you a glass of water," Julianna says. "Sit!" she orders.

I drag the chair and sit, my head still spinning. It's hard to breathe. Julianna puts a glass of water in front of me and pulls another chair. "First, you need to calm down," she says.

I inhale deeply, exhale slowly, then drink some water.

"What are we going to do with him?" I ask, my voice hoarse.

Julianna thinks about it for a few moments.

"We can toss him down the mudslide a few blocks away. People get washed down in mudslides all the time; bodies are found down the ravine every day," she says determinedly.

"But the marking on his neck... his face... when he's found, it won't look like drowning."

"And who exactly is going to investigate it? The District Police, whatever is left of it? Useless bunch of lazy clowns."

"He'll be missed at work," I whisper.

"Nah. People often stop showing up for work. They either find something else or they're dead."

"A parent?"

Julianna holds a stone-hard stare into my eyes. "Don't go soft on me, Juniper," she says. "He got what he deserved. You need to toughen up."

I nod absent-mindedly as I look at him, on the floor. His neck is almost purple, his face smashed and covered in blood. I can't believe only this morning we were all at work together.

"We'll carry him together when it's completely dark. I'll need to stay here tonight, though," Julianna says, and I nod quickly, relieved to have her company.

*

It's close to midnight. The neighbourhood is dark and quiet but for the sound of rain that keeps falling. Julianna and I drag the body out of the house, then we carry him. He's so heavy. She holds his torso; I hold the feet. I feel sick at the look of him. We take a few steps, then drop him down, unceremoniously, and rest. My back and arms are already hurting. On the ground, his face is swallowed up by the mud. It's such a grotesque sight. I can't avoid thinking of Enav, my brother. That's how he died. Choked by mud. When we received the news, a few hours later, Tui got almost hysterical. After losing her dad, her sister and then Rāwiri, her uncle's death really got to her. But out of that, suddenly grew a formidable determination not to give in. To live. I must do the same.

We pick him up again, swearing as we do. He feels even heavier now, and he's slippery from the mud. We nearly drop him again. Slowly, we make our way towards the most recently formed, and most active, mudslide.

Brown, murky water mixed with shrubs and earth, keep sliding down the path that is already well-formed in the soil. Down below us is a dark abyss, gushing menacingly.

The closer we get, the deeper the mud is. We sink deeper and deeper until it's no use. We might find ourselves sliding down too if we don't stop.

"We have to just push him down from here," Julianna says. "I reckon it's close enough, he'll get swallowed by the mud down the ravine."

The man already looks like an elongated mud cake. There is no trace of face, no features. We push him forward, from his feet, further and further towards the tip, until finally the slip claims him, and he's gone.

*

We make our way back to the house, drenched, and covered in mud from head to toe. My body is aching, my head still pounding, and between my legs there is a burning soreness.

As we barge through the door, we're welcomed by screams of fright. It takes a few seconds for Tui to realise the caked strangers who walked in so late at night were Julianna and me.

"What the heck, Mum? Where have you been? Why are you covered in mud?"

I'm so tired, I'm almost driven to simply tell her the truth and be done with it, but Julianna speaks first.

"We were afraid a mudslide was forming too close to the house, so we went to check."

"And?" Tui asks, alarmed.

"No, it's OK, no reason to be worried at this point," she replies.

"OK. I just, I came home, and you weren't home, Mum, and there was some blood on the floor, I was so scared!"

"Oh, I cut my hand, it's nothing," Julianna beats me to it, showing Tui her string cuts.

Tui seems to accept Julianna's stories, albeit with some reluctance. She still looks at me with those big, inquisitive eyes of hers, and I suspect she's trying to explain to herself what Julianna was doing here in the first place.

"Julianna came to give me a pair of her shoes, since mine were ripped. We had a lovely time, talking, and then it was just too late for her to go back home. It's not safe."

Tui nods slowly.

"But where have *you* been, Tui? You weren't home when I came back from work, I never know where you are, coming home after midnight…"

"I was with friends. I'm always with friends, they pick me up, they bring me home," she says, suddenly short of temper.

"Who? Which friends?"

"The ones I always hang out with. There's my friend Meva and a bunch of others. Why are you suddenly so concerned?"

"Because I worry. Because it's not safe out there."

"I'm fine. I'm never alone," Tui says.

I have to trust her. I couldn't lock her in this house even if I wanted to, and I don't want to. It's not safe outside, but if I've learned one thing today, it is that it isn't safe inside either. Nowhere is safe anymore. It hasn't been safe for years.

"OK," I say. I'm too tired to give it any more thought anyway.

I have to wash myself. There is no shower, no running water. I take the washcloth and scrub myself until my skin is red. I dunk my entire head in the copper tub and scrub my hair until it hurts.

When I'm done, Julianna, still coated by a thick layer of mud, sends me to bed. "I'll sort out the washing tub for myself, don't worry. You need to sleep."

I can hear her outside, spilling my bath water and refilling the tub with fresh rainwater from the water tank. I try to drift into sleep, reassured by the sense of safety Julianna and Tui give me.

*

It's late at night, or more precisely, early morning. Julianna is asleep on the makeshift sofa, and Tui in her room.

I can't sleep.

Visions of what had happened here only hours ago flash through my mind over and over. I can still feel his weight on my body. There is soreness between my legs. I still feel sick. My mind drifts to the sight of him, swollen by the mud. I can't help but bring up the image of Enav. I went to see him, after he was killed. He was working in the quarry. Sandbags and heavy stones have become such in-demand commodities, to defend against slips, spills, floods, and winds. The quarry was always looking for able-bodied, working men. Enav, my gentle brother, who grew up dreaming to be a marine biologist or an opera singer, was grinding his body every day, to make a living. The sudden flood came when he was deep in one of the remote areas of the dig. He was taken by the mud and drowned instantly, with all his eleven colleagues. I stood over his body in the small quarry mortuary; so often were they burying their men, they had their own death palace. My sweet big brother, he was covered in mud. I wept as I wiped and cleaned him with a piece of wet cloth, but the mud was within him, in his mouth, in his eyes; like a golem who failed to rise.

Tears slide down my face as I think about Enav, and again the thoughts take me back to Declan. The memory of his hands in my hair brings a new sense of disgust. More than him claiming my body for himself, the way he touched my hair as he did it, that false intimacy that he forced on me, enrages me.

There is such burning ache inside me, I want to scream it out, but I know I must swallow it, forever. Instead, I get out of bed and silently walk towards the washroom. The small room is dark, but I know my way around it. A box of matches is waiting on the shelf, and I use it to light the small, half-used candle in the corner. A warm glow reveals the wonky mirror-cabinet on the wall, above the small copper bowl we use as a basin. I open it. I find what I'm looking for amid a pile of wash cloths, Rāwiri's long-expired, old medicine bottles that I'm never going to throw away, some wooden toothbrushes and the jar of teeth cleaning ointment. I reach my hand and pick up the sharp scissors. There's a weird shine to them in the candlelight. Without hesitation, not bothering to look at my reflection in the mirror, I chop off all my hair.

Thirteen

I must talk to Julianna.

It's been nearly four months since that night. My changed hairstyle has caused more hushed murmurs than Declan's absence. In the end, just like Julianna had predicted, no one truly cared. I still pause every day by the makeshift "missing persons" board on my way to the bus station, but no one has put his image up yet. Maybe he had no one. So many people have lost their entire support circle.

I hold her back as we step down off the bus, letting everyone else pass us and disappear into the dam office.

"Everything OK?" she asks me.

I try to sort out the words, to spill it out without sounding too distraught.

"I'm pregnant," I whisper.

"What?"

I couldn't quite believe it myself. Not the fact that I was pregnant, but that it took me this long to figure it out. Like some clueless teenager.

"I thought I was menopausal. My period bleeds were playing up for a long time, and then stopped for a few months. I didn't think it was still possible," I say, confused, full of shame.

I've sensed that I was gaining weight, but it really wasn't all that much. It was only that morning, when Tui hugged me goodbye before I left, and she blurted out suddenly, 'What's up with your boobs, Mum? They're becoming ginormous!' that finally the penny dropped. Suddenly the weight gain, the filling of the breasts, the soreness, the occasional nausea, especially in the morning, all made sense.

Julianna looks at me kindly. "What are you going to do about it?" she asks.

I'd thought about it from the second I realised. It was Declan's child. Fruit of pain and humiliation. I didn't want it. I didn't feel I could love it. I certainly didn't have enough to feed it or look after it. The world was not suited for young ones anymore.

"I must get rid of it, Julianna," I say.

She nods.

I knew Julianna would know what to do. She had told me about ridding herself of a couple of what she called 'unfortunate accidents' before.

"My accidents weren't four months old," she says carefully. "I don't know if my special tea would help you, and if it does, what it might do to you."

"I don't care. Please. Can you make it for me?" I beg.

Some more people arrive at the dam, dispatches of a later bus. We join them and walk inside.

Fourteen

I stare at the deep green concoction that's in the mug in front of me. Julianna is with me, holding my hand.

"What's in it?" I ask.

"Oh, all sorts of things. Feverfew, meadowsweet, ginko, wild nettles, and some other stuff."

I wonder what the 'other stuff' is, and if it's going to kill me.

"Drink it in small sips," she advises me.

I raise the mug to my lips and start sipping. The flavour is bitter, earthy, and quite awful.

"You didn't expect it to taste good, I hope," Julianna chuckles at the sight of me gagging.

I'm so revolted by the flavour; a mist of tears clouds my eyes. I sigh loudly with every further gulp; my fingers claw into my thigh. Eventually the mug is emptied.

"How long before it starts working?" I ask.

"A few hours." Julianna takes the mug to the sink and gives it a quick wash. "I suggest you go lie down. It's going to be a rough night."

I'm so grateful for having her here. Grateful for her friendship.

*

I met Julianna on the same day I met Rāwiri. We bumped into each other—actually bumped into each other—while shopping for fruit at the monthly market, before it, too, closed down. There was something instant between us, a strike of immediate mutual fondness. It was so easy to be her friend. In a way, it was also assisted by the refreshing and comforting revelation that human connection was still possible. That random strangers could still become fast friends and love each other. Julianna has been my rock through so many disasters: Rāwiri's succumbing to the disease that was eating him up from the inside; Enav's traumatic drowning; my attack; not to mention the countless times she helped me financially, helped me survive. She's the closest person to me, other than Tui, probably closer than Tāne.

*

The pain has been coming up in waves this past hour and it's excruciating. I'm sweating so heavily; the pillow is now completely soaked and sticky.

"How are you holding up?" Julianna comes in to check on me, offering me some water to drink.

"It's like he's attacking me all over again," I moan, a bolt of pain shatters through my abdomen and lower back.

She seems concerned. "I need to check between your legs, love," she says, matter-of-factly. I toss the sheets away and let her check me.

It's a bit late for modesty, given the circumstances.

"Soon enough you'll need to start pushing," she says. "You may want to start walking around, it could help."

I try to push myself off the bed, but another pain shoots up my spine. I sit it out, crunching my teeth, then rise on my feet. Even though my belly isn't big, it feels heavy, and I'm moved to put both my hands under it, as if carrying a large load. I walk to the kitchen bench and back. Then to Tui's room and back. Tui is conveniently staying at her friend Meva's place overnight, which is why I asked Julianna to come and have it done here. The other option was having it done at Julianna's, but I preferred the familiarity of my own space. The space that was defiled by that man, whose mark I was now trying to rid myself of. But it was still my space.

This house had already been scarred by sad memories. Rāwiri's decline from cancer, long nights of pain and delirium, of nursing him, of listening to him cry, of cleaning him and then, cleaning after he'd gone, it happened right here, within these walls. As I drag myself from wall to wall, I wonder if any of it would have happened if Rāwiri were still here. It could have. Him being late from work, the scene could have played out in the exact same way. What would he have felt about this baby that was growing inside me? I can't answer that. Rāwiri was immensely kind, but this was such a shattering situation, I wouldn't have wanted to test him with it.

I suddenly have a great need to go and relieve myself in the toilet hole. Julianna stops me in my tracks.

"Don't use the sanitised hole! Use a bucket." She hurries and grabs a bucket from the washroom.

"Here, use this," she says as she positions the bucket underneath me. "This is a good sign, Juniper. It could be the foetus coming out."

I look at her, tired, clouded with pain and exhaustion.

"Here, let me help you," she holds my hands and counterbalances my body weight as I crouch over the bucket.

To my surprise and relief, the foetus slides out into the bucket. Seeing the little body in the bucket, covered in uterus slime and blood, makes me shudder, and suddenly I'm flooded with tears. I burst into a loud sob. I cry out all the pain and the sorrow that were shut inside me since that night. My body shakes, as I heave with such a cocktail of emotions, and with the sudden rush of hormonal release.

"Wait!" Julianna says as she kneels at my feet and places each of her hands on the side of my legs, just above the ankles, each hand clutching tightly, pushing hard and rubbing. "We need to get the placenta out," she explains. "Now, push!"

Like magic, it slides out within a few short moments. I don't know how she knows to do all that. I'll ask her one day, after this is all over and done with.

We stand above the bucket in silence.

"Do you want to say anything?" Julianna asks tenderly.

I take a moment, trying to steady my thoughts, my breaths.

"I'm sorry, little one," I say finally, and Julianna covers the bucket with a towel.

She helps me clean up, changes my sheets, then lays me back in bed. I feel under my pillow for the two pieces of paper I hid there. The letter to Tui, and Rāwiri's poem. Did Juliana move them when she changed the bedding? My heart races, until my fingers sense the old, folded papers with a touch. I still have them.

"Try to sleep. I'll bury her," she says.

Fifteen

"Have you told Tui yet?" Julianna asks me.

We're on our lunch break, sitting at our usual place. I'm still quite sore and hormonal. I only took two days off work. Had I taken more, I would not have had a job to go back to. There was no social security, no health care to speak of. Everyone needed the money. Everyone. Miss more than a couple of days, and there's a queue of people ready and willing to replace you at the door, even for specialised office work like mine, where some education is still required.

"No," I reply.

I don't think I'll ever tell her if I'm honest. There are things I'd rather she simply didn't know—about me, about the world. I needed to remain that person she looks up to, to help her, to advise her, to save her—not the victim, not the killer that I've turned out to be.

The killer.

I try not to think about it. Every day, I do my best to block it completely out of my mind, to shut down all possible emotions and thoughts linked to the past four months. There are days when I succeed, other days I feel as if I'm about to collapse, shatter into a million little pieces and never recover.

"*He* did this to you," Julianna reads my mind. "*He* did." She reaches for my hand, grabs it, and squeezes it. "Nothing that has happened was your choice, or your fault!"

I smile at her, a sad little smile, but one which I hope conveys I'm grateful.

"I'm so tired of being the victim," I manage to say, after a short and painful silence.

"Aren't we all?" Julianna responds.

*

The sudden loud burst of the emergency alarm makes us all jump out of our seats. No earthquakes or dramatic landslips have preceded it this time. Curious and a little confused, we obey protocol and leave the office in an orderly fashion, congregating outside, in the pouring rain, eagerly speculating at what it was that caused this.

They found his body, I tell myself, my heart beating so hard, I might faint. *They know.*

The dayshift manager finally joins us outside, looking grim.

"Folks, I'm sorry but I have some awful news to share with you, and I know that you'll take it hard, because we're all colleagues here, and we all share hours and days working together in this great place."

This is it.

"I don't know if you've heard, but the terrorist group Climate Revenge, has struck down at the heart of our parent company, Oxy-mask Limited."

It takes me a few seconds to register what he's saying. So, this is not about Declan? This is about some terrorist group. What did he say that they did? I completely missed it.

"A bomb went off at the heart of Oxy-mask a couple of nights ago," he says.

"So why tell us now?" someone shouts from the back.

"Ah, because only now the damage has been made clear, and it's considerable. Maybe, I mean probably irreparable."

I'm still waiting for the punch line. What does all of that have to do with us?

"I believe you're all aware that Oxy-mask part-owns Future Planet, which owns this dam, so..." he coughs an insincere cough, "erm, a hit on Oxy-mask is a hit on us."

"Get to the point, Michael!" Someone at the back is obviously losing patience.

"We're closing down the dam," he blurts finally, and a wave of disgruntled accusations gushes towards him. Quickly he adds, "It's not like we were meant to go on indefinitely here. This work had a deadline from the very beginning, we're just bringing the deadline closer, that's all."

"How long do we have?" another voice asks.

"A week."

"We can't finish all the work in one week!" a man shouts from the back.

The dayshift manager, Michael, pauses for quite some time before he finally says, "Folks, uh, we're... so, we'll get specialised Oxy-mask contractors to finish the job. Seems like the company believes these people can do it within seven days."

Loud protests ensue. Julianna and I look at each other. We know arguing will make not a shred of a difference.

"It's Oxy-mask's decision, it's out of my hands," Michael says.

"You can't do that!" There are shouts.

"These jobs are our livelihoods!" a woman at the back adds.

"We need to eat!"

"Yeah!" people murmur in agreement.

"There are no other jobs! You're throwing us to the street!"

"Yeah!"

"Folks, please," Michael says, "it's not like we were going to stay open forever, this site was about to close!"

"But you gave us no time to prepare! You said we have six months!"

"I want to be paid for the full six months!"

"Yeah!" people shout in unison. "We want to be paid in full!"

There is a charged anger that runs through the crowd like electricity. People at the back start pushing the people in front of them to move forward, and they push the ones in front of them, like a wave. A stampede is brewing.

Michael starts retreating towards the entrance.

"I can't authorise that, I'm sorry. It's out of my hands," he keeps saying.

"How much do they pay you, Michael? Bet they're keeping you here!"

I feel that I'm being pushed forward and am squashed against the people in front of me, sandwiched between them and the people behind me. I don't want to participate in whatever this is becoming. People are so angry and resentful; I don't know what they might do. Someone might get hurt, and it's not going to make any difference whatsoever.

I grab Julianna's hand and start squeezing my way sideways, out, and away from the raw build-up of violent intent that pulses within this congregation. I manage to pull us both out and we take several good steps to distance ourselves from the rest, along with several other employees, mainly from the office.

It's only seconds before there's a charge on the front doors by the masses. Michael manages to get inside but he fails to lock the door before the crowd reaches in. I can see him being toppled over and trampled under angry feet.

I'm not sure what these people are going to do. It might end up with the dam managers being hanged, drawn, and quartered. I wouldn't be surprised if it does. I'd witnessed violence I couldn't have imagined would take place in my lifetime, yet it did. Maybe humans aren't capable of life without cruel brutality. The more history moves onwards, the more we step backwards. We brought our own catastrophe upon ourselves.

"Let's get out of here," Julianna whispers in my ears. "This will end very badly."

I nod. I don't want to witness this.

*

"Don't worry," Julianna says when we're finally on the bus. "I may have something for us instead of this job."

"What is it?" I ask.

"My boyfriend's friend, from when they were both in the army, he mentioned that they need helpers at his military base," she says.

"Doing what?" I wonder.

"Same as here, filing, accounts. Something about armament tracing, weapon recovery, that sort of stuff."

"Don't you need to be a soldier for this kind of work?"

"No one is enlisted anymore. It's a job," Julianna says.

I nod. "Yeah, OK."

There was always a lifeline from Julianna, my one and only friend.

*

I walk home briskly from the bus stop, turning my head back every few seconds, making sure no one is following me. There's no one behind me.

I keep thinking about what might be happening right now at the dam. It's inconceivable, how people you work with every single day, spend hours with, share a lunch with, can turn on you in a second, as Declan did with me, as these people did with Michael, and probably all the other managers.

In my head, I'm going over everything Michael had said. It was out of his hands. I'm sure it was. He was a victim of this bad decision just as much as all the other employees were. I feel so sad for him.

What did he say happened at Oxy-mask? A bomb, I think he said. Placed by the Climate Revenge group. He called them terrorists. I don't feel like they warranted that title. I suppose those with the cash, those who have the most to lose from such groups—groups of individuals who are passionate and desperate for change—they feel the most entitled, and most ready to bestow titles such as 'terrorists'.

The more I think about it, climbing up the muddy hill to my house, the more the title 'terrorists' angers me. How dare they, all the money-grabbers that still exist in this broken world, lay the blame at the doorstep of others?

All those rich conglomerates, smug politicians, aloof decision-makers, and policy-setters, when they had the chance to act—they failed us all. For years they avoided targeting the real problem, which was animal agriculture. The world was repeatedly warned by scientists and environmentalists, telling us clearly and forcefully, that it was the single biggest climate-threatening problem to solve. It caused methane pollution of the atmosphere, and nitrate pollution of freshwater and groundwater. It was the driving force behind deforestation and the loss of biodiversity. Most wasteful in terms of land and water use. Above all else, it was a violent food system, and deeply immoral.

But all those leaders had preferred inaction over angering the animal agriculture sector. For years they neglected to act. Instead, they invested and made even more money from providing us haphazard solutions, such as expensive personal oxygen masks. Solutions we wouldn't have needed, if only our leaders did the right thing at the right time. Is it any wonder there are those who rise to action?

I feel quite strongly that if I were younger, say, Tui's age, I would have been part of those groups. It's what Mum would've wanted, for sure.

The thought makes me stop in my tracks. I feel strangely warm, suddenly, and a little lightheaded. Tui. Of course, Tui. All the sneaking around, disappearing late at night and sometimes overnight. She'd always been political, admiring Climate Revenge since she was a young teen. I didn't think much of it when I found those posters in her room, but she must have been part of it.

The realisation that this had to be so, comes to me so profoundly and so clearly that I don't even need to ask her. I just know. She never said anything, but I know.

We all now have our secrets.

FIVE

YEARS

EARLIER:

2053

Sixteen

I think I'm far enough away from the house to make this call. I don't want Rāwiri to see me.

I know Rāwiri is ill, and it churns my guts with worry. I know he knows he's ill, he's a medical doctor after all. True, when he was still practicing, his field was dermatology, but he has all the necessary knowledge of a professional to know that his body is failing him, deteriorating from within at worrying speed.

I know he knows that I know. It's in his eyes.

I must talk to the district General Practitioner, Dr Schubert. He's the only one left in our area still consulting. Everyone else has either left or died. It's a matter of two and a half hours of rough driving to get to the clinic. Rāwiri has given his beaten old car to his son, Tāne, and I dare not ask either of them to go. None of us has opened up the subject, yet.

I can't force Rāwiri to come with me, but I have the number to call, and I have the satellite phone. The only kind of phones still working, until, I suppose, the satellites start decomposing in space too.

I pick a sheltered spot behind a curve in the road, where I can't be spotted from any of the houses in our street. A pathetic row of assembled abodes, that people still did their best to maintain. It is quite humid, but the sun has finally come out, and the last few days have been so lovely. Days like these are like magic. They instantly remind me of The Before. Memories of my childhood flood me. Happy days by the seaside, with Enav, doing beach clean-ups and crab spotting, coming home with red cheeks and salty hair. It is incredible to observe how life responds to this welcomed change in the weather so eagerly. On days like these, when the heat and the sunlight dry up the mud, and buds of wildflowers waste no time stretching themselves upwards and prepare to quickly bloom, when people you randomly meet suddenly smile, or even say a non-committal 'hello'. Days like these make all the difference. They dry out the tired and beaten soul and instil hope and optimism in its stead.

But those are always short lived.

I dial the number scribbled on a note, almost surprised to hear the dialling tone.

"Hello?" A female voice. Expecting to hear Dr Schubert, I'm taken aback.

"Oh, hi," I mumble. "Is this Dr Schubert's office?"

"You'll have to speak up louder, dear," the woman says.

I suppose the satellites don't pass over this spot very often.

"Hi," I shout into the speaker, "is this Dr Schubert's office?"

"Yes, dear," the woman responds. I don't know how I feel about being called 'dear'. There is something very old-fashioned about it, a little out of date, a little out of place. Kind of endearing yet somewhat, I don't know, patronising. She can't be that much older than I am, but called 'dear', I feel like a child.

"I need to speak to him, please," I tell the woman, who I assume to be the doctor's wife, rather than an assistant.

"And who shall I say is calling?" she asks.

"This is Juniper Hawthorn, I'm the partner of Dr Rāwiri Kent, he's an old friend of Dr Schubert," I reply, trying to sound friendly and encouraging, anything so that she doesn't hang up on me.

"Oh yes, Rāwiri, I remember him," she says, her voice full of obvious fondness. "How is he?"

"Well... erm, this is what I wanted to discuss with Dr Schubert," I manage to mumble.

"Oh, of course, dear. Let me see if he's available," she says and disappears.

I can feel the seconds tick away in my bones. Soon Rāwiri will be wondering where I disappeared to. I'm so afraid of raising this subject with him. I feel as if, once I say these words, once I utter them in speech, then amorphic concepts of sickness become concrete. Spoken, it will all become real.

"Hello, are you there?" the woman's voice returns, and I hold my breath.

"Yes, I'm here."

"Oh, I'm so sorry, Juniper dear, but Dr Schubert is currently with patients. He says he'll call you back later if that's OK?"

That would be the worst possible thing to happen. What if he calls and Rāwiri picks up? I'll need to hide the phone, I need to silence its ringing, I need to throw it away, drown it in water, I need to—

"Yes, of course. Thank you so much!"

I turn off the call. My ear is already red and hot, baked by the old phone. God knows what brain damage this was doing me, projecting my braincells to ancient satellites in space.

I can't help walking home with a heavy heart. I was hoping to gain some reassurance, some ideas on how to address this, some confidence that there are still treatments available, somewhere, that people who are not excessively rich could afford.

We've only been together four years, Rāwiri and me, yet it seemed so much longer. His right hand over my shoulder, pressing me against him below that hairy underarm niche, where I could lean onto him, spoon, and hug, feel his warmth and sense his breath, that has felt like the safest place in the entire world. He was fifteen years my senior, and possibly the kindest man I'd ever met. In a funny twist of events, I met both him and Julianna on the same day, the two of them soon becoming the most formidable pillars of strength in my life.

*

It was one of those surprising, pleasant weather days, when the three of us happened upon the same monthly fruit and vegetable market. The market used to be a bustling magnet for shoppers, held every Sunday in The Before, at the centre of town. Now, however, the sea had claimed the entire trading area and much of the residential neighbourhoods around it; the Great Famine had cost so many lives and food was so scarce and hard to grow that the market had shrunk and moved higher up to a hilly part of the old town. What used to be an exciting space to buy sensually-appealing, mouth-watering crops, fruit, and herbs of the most alluring aromas, was reduced to just a few sad, sparse stalls, offering a small selection of whatever could be grown under the hostile new climate by those who still dug their heels in and kept trying.

There were fewer stalls each time, until eventually the market was no more, replaced by wealthy conglomerates, such as WeFeedU who grew our food underground or in huge, temperature-controlled, green-growing hubs. They'd invested multi-millions in the design of the technology alone, just to imitate weather conditions that occurred naturally on our planet, in The Before. These designer fruits and vegetables on offer now, tended to taste like cardboard and cost a small fortune. Eventually, the market was replaced by visiting pop-up stalls that moved from settlement to settlement. They visit our street every Tuesday.

That pleasant day on the monthly market, I settled for several potatoes, a cucumber that looked a bit mouldy (but, gosh, I missed the flavour of cucumber), and an outrageously expensive kilo of bananas. I thought I'd surprise Tui with the bananas. On the rare occasion when I managed to put my hands on them, Tui was ecstatic, stuffing herself to constipation. She was only ten then, my Tui. I tried to haggle buying only half the bunch, but the grower, an unpleasant woman who had no intention to compromise, wouldn't have a bar of it.

"One kilo bunch or move away."

My hands were shaking when I handed her the notes. I was already contemplating what to cut out that month when the grower's assistant, a younger woman who was only watching from the side until then, suddenly said, "Juniper?"

I looked at her. She seemed very familiar, but I just couldn't place her. I had no connections within the growers' community and wasn't expecting to know anyone at the market.

"Yes?" I answered, searching my memory, trying to remember where I might know her from.

"I'm Aisha," the woman said, and my mouth dropped to the floor.

"Aisha?"

"Yes. How are you? It's been…"

"Decades!" I replied.

Assisting a banana grower on the monthly market was not where I'd expect to reunite with Aisha, my old childhood friend. My best friend. We spent the year between almost-fourteen to almost-fifteen constantly in each other's company. My heart broke when she left to live with her grandmother, after a tragedy in her family. I wouldn't have recognised her if she hadn't told me her name. Her sleek, long brown hair was cut short and almost completely grey, her chic glasses replaced with plain frames, and her lovely face looked unnaturally swollen, like the face my mum had when she was medicated.

"What are you doing here?" I asked her.

"I'm helping my in-laws," she replied, with an almost apologetic tone.

So, she married into this growers' family. This sour woman was her mother-in-law. I suddenly felt sorry for her.

She smiled at me, I smiled back.

But it wasn't genuine. There was something very sad about meeting someone who was intensely dear to me, many years back, yet suddenly, I found that I just didn't know what to say to her. The magic we'd shared, it faded a long time ago. Our lives took different paths, and mine crossed so many minefields, it changed me. I wasn't looking to rekindle something that belonged in a life that no longer existed.

"Well, it was nice to see you again," she said.

"You too," I replied, and turned to walk away, as fast as possible.

I wasn't really watching where I was going, when I bumped into a woman, knocking her to the ground.

"I'm so sorry!" I gushed, immediately offering my hand to help her up.

"I think I twisted my ankle," she said groaning, barely managing to lift herself from the ground.

She looked well kept, in her floaty floral blouse and shiny black trousers, strawberry-blonde hair in a stylish hairdo, and she smelled so good; I could smell her lovely perfume from where I stood above her. As one who didn't put quite as much effort into my appearance and odour just for going to the market, I was impressed.

"I'm so sorry," I kept saying to her. 'Here, let me help you to the bench."

She leaned on my arm and hobbled towards one of the few wooden benches that weren't taken. I leaned to take a look at her ankle. Her foot was stylishly pedicured, her toes embellished with red polish, her sandals delicate. A silver anklet embraced her sore ankle; it didn't seem swollen.

"Don't worry, it happens to me sometimes," the woman said. "It will be fine in a few days." She smiled whimsically and added, "I just need to find a good, strong man to carry me for a while."

There was something very disarming and engaging about this woman. I think I must have instantly liked her. I smiled back.

"Why don't you have it checked by a doctor?" I asked.

"I don't know any doctors," she replied.

"I'm a doctor," a man, sitting on the bench next to us said.

"There you go," I said. "Found one for you."

"I'm afraid I'm not the kind of doctor you need, though," the man quickly added.

"Let me guess," the woman said, clearly entertained, "you're a Doctor of Philosophy. Or is it theology? No. I'm guessing, engineering?"

"No, no, I'm a medical doctor, but not the kind you need," the man apologised. "I'm a dermatologist. But I can certainly bandage a foot!"

I was wondering what he could use for a bandage, when the woman offered a floral scarf, she had in her bag.

"No need, I always travel with some medical basics," the man said, and took a white bandage out of his bag, tightly rolled.

The woman and I exchanged quick looks. I think we both were thinking *what a find*. He kneeled at the woman's foot, taking off the anklet and handing it to the woman, before he started applying the bandage.

"It's beautiful," I said, looking at the piece of jewellery still in her hand. It looked exquisite.

"Thank you," the woman said. "It's only a fake; I wouldn't dare wear real jewels out in public nowadays. You could easily get murdered for it."

I nodded, wondering how a potential mugger might know the difference between real and fake jewels, when the woman added, "It's a sad situation. Until about ten years ago I used to be a jewellery designer, and quite famous even."

I knew she looked familiar!

"Are you Julianna De Agostini?" I gushed at the woman.

"Yes, that is me," she said with a smile.

Wow. A proper celebrity.

I watched the doctor with great interest. He was tall and lean, his thick dark hair greying in parts, his face handsome, but not in the too-handsome way. He had the look of someone you immediately wanted to trust. Suddenly, he raised his eyes and looked at me. The power created by the locking together of our eyes nearly blew me off the bench.

"There, all done. Please take it easy on that foot for the next few days," he said.

"Sure I can't use your services carrying me around, Doctor?" Julianna asked with a cheeky smile.

"I'm afraid it's not my specialty either," he said with an apologetic smile, sneaking a quick glance at me. I could sense myself blushing like a little girl.

"Oh, what a shame," she laughed, putting her huge sunglasses on.

"What's your name?" she suddenly asked me.

"Juniper," I said, and shook her hand. Her handshake was firm and confident.

"It was such a joy meeting you, Juniper. Let's meet here again next month, shall we?"

She tried to get up but was clearly still sore. I jumped up to steady her on her feet.

"Please, Julianna, let me compensate you," I was quick to say, perhaps too quick, as I took the bananas out of my shopping bag and handed them over to her.

"No, I can't take your bananas, they're too expensive."

"Please. It's the only way I can make all this up to you."

She took the bananas, and while I gave them to her wholeheartedly and willingly, it actually hurt my heart to see them disappear into her bag, along with the money I paid and Tui's shrieks of joy.

"Meet me here next month," she said again, squeezing my shoulder with obvious fondness. "And thank you, Doctor....?" she said, raising her last syllable, clearly indicating an expectancy for him to say his name.

"Rāwiri. Dr Rāwiri Kent."

She smiled at us and disappeared. I could imagine a fancy limousine waiting for her, hiding somewhere. Only the following month, when we met, did I realise that she actually took the bus, that she had lost quite a bit of the incredible wealth she used to have before her jewellery business closed down, and that she was a most down to earth, friendly, and wonderful person. We hit it off immediately and never looked back.

The doctor had disappeared into the crowd, and I quickly realised that I'd spent all my money on those bananas, and there was nothing left for the bus. I had to walk home.

"Juniper, wait!" someone called after me.

I was surprised and pleased to see it was him. In his hand he held a huge bunch of bananas, bigger and nicer by far than those I purchased earlier from Aisha's mother-in-law.

"Here, I got them for you. I know those bananas cost you plenty, and you gave them to Julianna anyway. That means you are a very kind woman. Kind, and very beautiful, if I may."

I smiled, feeling surprised and flattered.

"Please, take them."

I took them. He walked me home. We were inseparable since.

Seventeen

I'm back at the house. Rāwiri has put an old record on, so the power must be on. Electricity has become exceedingly precarious in the past months, along with pretty much everything else that was failing and falling apart all over. I recognise the music. It's 'Death and Transfiguration' by the composer Richard Strauss. I remember the first time he played this record to me. I close my eyes and let the music engulf me, immerse me. It is emotive, powerful. I could feel it penetrate every cell of my skin; I could inhale it, into the smallest membrane of my lungs. There was struggle in this music, there was loss. Suddenly, the selection of this particular musical piece by Rāwiri seems to me to be ominous and deeply worrying.

I walk in, trying to hide the phone in my hand.

"Mum," Tui runs over to me, "have you heard? Climate Revenge said they'd blow the stupid dam up!'"

"Who?"

"Climate Revenge!" she says in such an incredulous tone. "Only the most influential and powerful climate justice activist group there is!" and with that, she disappears into her room, the way teenagers do.

I place the phone on the cabinet, where it usually sits, hoping Rāwiri hasn't noticed I took it. He is cutting turnips and onions. Something is already cooking, and the smell is divine. He's such a fantastic cook. I walk over to him and place my hand on his strong back. He turns his head towards me and smiles.

Say it. Say it. Say it. Say it.

"We need to talk, Rāwiri."

He puts down the knife and turns to me, looking worried.

"Now?"

His eyes are deep brown, his voice so warm, it takes the littlest gesture by him to make me burst with love. I lose my courage. How can I discuss illness and death with him now? I can't bring myself to visualise a life without him.

"Maybe after dinner?" I suggest. *Coward.*

He nods. "Here, peel those potatoes," he says.

I enjoy the next few minutes of standing next to him, preparing dinner together, listening to Strauss, pretending nothing is wrong.

*

We're seated at the table when the phone rings. Dammit, I forgot to silence it, or throw it out, or drown it.

Rāwiri, looking surprised, walks over to the cabinet and picks it up. I can feel my heart beating at triple speed.

"Hello? Oh, Jerry my friend, it's been a long time, what brings you to call? A-huh. A-huh... Oh I see... Yes... A-huh... She did? A-

104

huh…"

He glances at me with a sad look as he takes the phone to continue his conversation in the bedroom. He comes out, still on the phone, but clearly at the tail end of it. "See you on Thursday, my friend, yes," and he turns off the call.

When he's back at the table he looks different, defeated.

"Who was that?" Tui asks, clueless.

"Oh, just an old friend," Rāwiri says, looking at me.

*

"Why didn't you come to me first?" he asks me softly when we are finally alone.

"Why didn't you say anything?" I answer.

He sighs. "It took me a while to come to terms with it myself," he grabs my hand in his hand, "I know I'm sick. It's probably cancer. I am powerless to stop it," he sighs. "I know how it feels to lose someone to a prolonged disease," he says, referring to his late wife who died a decade earlier. "So does Tāne. It isn't pretty."

I know how it feels too.

"But there must be things that you can do?" I ask with desperation.

"There might be medication that can help slow it down," he nods. "I'm sorry I didn't open this subject with you. I couldn't. It was easier to pretend everything was normal."

Tears start to prick my eyes.

"I don't blame you for calling Jerry," he smiles kindly, as the tears dislodge from the rim of my eyes and roll down my cheeks. "I doubt there's much he could do either, but I made an appointment to see him, on Thursday."

I inhale with some relief.

"I'll ask Tāne for the car. It would be a good opportunity to tell him as well."

I nod.

"While we're there we could visit your brother, Enav, if you want? The quarry isn't that far away from the clinic."

I rejoice at the thought of seeing Enav again. I always thought of the quarry as being somewhere at the end of the world, but I guess, so is the clinic. "Sure, that would be nice," I say, "but let's not tell Tui anything yet."

He nods.

Eighteen

As if the visit to Dr Schubert's clinic wasn't hard enough, I'm deeply troubled by the conditions of Enav's living. It's no more than a cubby hole for grown men. There is barely space for the extra chair that he drags in for us. In addition to the narrow mattress, the small desk, and the chair already in there, there is room for nothing else. Located in a dormitory compound within the quarry-owned grounds, the place is smelly, with very little privacy. Enav has aged, his hair is thinning, his gentle facial features have hardened, his eyes are sunken. He hugs me long and hard. "So good to see you, Sis."

I understand the kind of desperation, and depression, that led Enav on the sad path to being here, but my heart breaks for him. There is such despondency in this place.

"I'm sorry, I can't offer you anything to eat. They don't allow us that sort of thing," he apologises.

"It's alright," Rāwiri reassures him, "we've eaten."

*

We had to stop somewhere after the visit to the clinic. Not to eat; on the contrary, I felt so queasy and sickened by that experience, it was unbearable to go on. An old inn, surprisingly still open for business, was the only option. The place stank of burned oil, which didn't help, and I rushed to the sanitised hole at the back. Thoughts of what we'd just experienced burned a hole in my stomach.

Dr Schubert's clinic was tiny, and already packed to the brim with people, many of them in a deep state of malnutrition. So many cases of young children, already displaying mouths abundant with rotting teeth, skin covered with open sores, the protruding bellies of prolonged starvation. It turns out Dr Schubert was not only providing whatever medicine he could in terms of pharmaceuticals; the most frequent medicine he provided the community was food. However, because food was in short supply, and hunger, combined with desperation, drive people to dangerous actions—as I tragically knew all too well—Dr Schubert would see his patients behind a barrier of heavy bars, wearing a protective bullet proof vest, which, I thought, couldn't help him should a possessed person aim at his head. He couldn't actually examine anyone properly, listen to heart beats, feel the softness of a tummy. It was all theoretical, and deeply, deeply disappointing.

Rāwiri and I were given priority, being old friends, that we felt embarrassed to accept, but Dr Schubert refused to see any other patients if we didn't accept his invite to go in promptly.

He was a short man with an almost completely bald head and a very bushy grey moustache. His equally bushy eyebrows looked like two wild bird nests, towering over his kind eyes that shone bright blue, hiding behind a pair of thick-framed glasses.

"There are often knives drawn in the waiting room," he said as a matter of explanation. "You don't want to be waiting out there."

"You're doing God's work here, Jerry," Rāwiri said, with deep respect, "giving these people food."

"The change happened organically,' Dr Schubert explained, "not necessarily by design." He gave a tired, narrow, half smile. "But it's true that, regardless, my heart won't let me close."

"How do you manage to maintain it? Where is the food coming from?"

"We have our donors. Not everyone is as desperate as these people. What you see here is really the worst of it... but there are many like them."

"I would like to become a donor, Jerry," Rāwiri said.

"Thank you, my friend, but it's not necessary. We have some wealthy patrons with a burning social conscience. Some from the nearby quarry. They foot the bill." He smiled one more of those narrow, tired, half smiles. "But how are you, Rāwiri? Some worrying signs, I understand?"

Rāwiri sneaked a look at me and nodded.

"What do you suspect?" Dr Schubert asked.

Rāwiri coughed before blurting, "Cancer. Stomach. Maybe colon."

Dr Schubert nodded slowly, sadly. "How long have you had symptoms?"

Rāwiri was silent for a while, then, quietly, apologetically, said, "Almost a year."

I could feel my breath lock inside me, being suddenly unable to either exhale or inhale. One year. One year of his sickness and I only noticed it a few weeks ago. And he didn't tell me.

Rāwiri, knowing what sort of a bomb he just dropped into the room, reached for my hand.

"Do you have anything I can take, Jerry? Oxaliplatin, Capecitabine?"

"No XELOX, I'm afraid. The only thing I can offer is Methotrexate."

Rāwiri inhaled deeply. "OK, that's OK."

"I'm really sorry, my friend," Dr Schubert whispered. "I wish I could help more."

*

I came out of the sanitised hole at the inn feeling even sicker than before. Rāwiri was seated at a table, set with a small bowl of greasy fried chips and two glasses filled with some unrecognisable home-brewed drinks.

"It's supposed to be beer," he smiled, "but I suspect it's water mixed with piss."

"Rāwiri…"

"Well, I had to try. Imagine it really was beer."

I sat at the table, sick to my stomach, yet hungry for those greasy potatoes. We ate in silence, then left for the quarry.

*

"So, how are you doing?" Rāwiri asks Enav, and I don't know which one of them looks worse or has aged less within a period of just a few months.

"Yeah, nah," Enav says, with some embarrassment, "it's the only job in miles. It's not like I had options."

"Why?" I blurt out, and there is some unexpected anger in my voice, percolating since the clinic, I suspect. "Why don't you have options? It's not like there is a family and children involved. You're not supporting anyone. Why are you here? Breaking your body? Holed in this tiny, stinky room? Is this some sort of self-punishment?"

"Juniper," Rāwiri tries to calm me down.

"You know that there was a family when I started here, Juniper, why are you saying that? It's cruel of you." Enav seems genuinely hurt.

"But that's happened. You can't change that, but you can change where you are, what you do!"

Enav takes a deep breath. "I can't move on from that, Juniper. I'm not like you. I don't have your strength. I can't. And I don't want to."

"So, you'll just work yourself into oblivion, is that it?"

"Yes. Yes, I guess you could say that," he replies defensively. "What's got into you? Why are you like that?"

He looks at me with so much pain, I feel his hurt like an invisible slap on my face. Why *am* I like that?

"Rāwiri has cancer." I blurt out what was blocked so hard inside me, and then burst into heaves of sobbing.

Both men jump to offer their support, but both are the cause of my misery, both project so much pain. The beloved soulmate, a rock of a man who is crumbling, and the gentle brother who would rather die under a rock than live with the memories of the life he once had.

"I'm sorry to hear it," Enav says softly. "Is it curable?"

"Maybe in The Before, if I was diagnosed in time, it could have been. But, not these days," Rāwiri answers sadly.

"We're right back in the Dark Ages, huh?" Enav says.

"Worse, I think," Rāwiri replies. "At least back in the Dark Ages, there was the Renaissance coming. I don't think we're going to be that lucky, this time."

"How long do you have?" Enav asks.

"I… I can't say," Rāwiri apologises softly.

We fall silent.

"Just like Mum," Enav says finally, quietly.

"Your mother died of cancer?" Rāwiri asks, and I realise I'd bolted it so tightly, deep inside me, I never told him. I should have told him.

"Yes," I reply, my voice still trembling. The memories of her extended decline left such a permanent scar on my soul, I can't bear to go through it all over again, yet it seems I must. "Breast cancer."

He nods, sadly. "I'm sorry."

"I was twenty. It was before the Great Famine. Maybe she did herself a favour, departing before the crux of the climate crisis," I say, wiping my eyes. "But she suffered, that's for sure. Even though she had hospital treatment and all, she suffered a lot." Memories of her wailing from pain, the sick that I had to clean, her perishing away, slowly. How could I go through it again, with Rāwiri?

"She loved you," Enav says.

"She loved you, too."

"Yes, but you could manipulate her in a way no one else could," he smiles. "Remember Johnny?"

I smile, genuinely. Johnny, the stray dog I brought home despite all her protestations and threats to throw him out. I knew she wouldn't. In the end we all fell in love with that mutt. He was part of our family.

"Our dog," he explains to Rāwiri. "Juniper was fourteen or fifteen then. Her soft heart wouldn't let her leave an abandoned animal behind."

"I can believe it," Rāwiri says kindly.

"She was fearless," Enav adds.

I don't remember ever being fearless. I'm surprised this is how he used to see me.

There's an ear-splitting ring in the hallway that makes Enav jump.

"Sorry, my shift is starting soon, I gotta go."

"Enav, why don't you come over to our place on Christmas?" Rāwiri asks. "Have Christmas with us. Tui would love to see you.

Tāne too. Stay for a few days. We don't have a lot of room, but… more than this."

"Yes, I'd love to," Enav says. "They let us have Christmas off, if we choose, without pay."

"Fantastic. I'll get Tāne to come and pick you up on Christmas Eve."

Nineteen

The table looks festive enough. I know we have nothing to complain about; we're doing better than so many others. I was able to buy a bit of wheat grain last week from the WeFeedU pop-up stall.

I was buying some extra potatoes, parsnips, and carrots for the Christmas dinner, when the stall operator whispered to me,

"Hey lady, are you interested in some grain?"

He asked it so silently, I couldn't understand what he was offering me, drugs? Heroin?

"What?" I asked.

He seemed alarmed, popped his head out of the service window and looked around, making sure I didn't draw other people's attention to his illicit activity.

"Grains. Wheat. You want some?"

He placed a small bag of grain on the counter. It had been a while since I'd seen grains of any shape or form. The Great Famine erased more than eighty-five percent of all grain crops worldwide. For all I knew, countries in Europe were still fighting each other for the little there was, rendering whole territories of dead-zones into warzones. These looked a bit too green, but I desired them so badly.

"How much?" I asked, and nearly lost my balance with the shock of the price tag.

Realising I was not going to pay what he just asked for, he immediately lowered the price. I wasn't trying to haggle, but he was obviously keen to sell. I ended up buying fewer carrots and more grain.

Rāwiri has managed to make flatbread with the grain I bought and has cooked the most mouth-watering potato and parsnip pie. Julianna, who is celebrating with us for the first time this year since breaking up with her most recent boyfriend (an artist who was too sombre for her), has brought a lovely bowl of wild leaf salad, and some baked potatoes; she has even managed to find a small punnet of strawberries.

"Strawberries!" Tui cries with delight. "Where did you get those?"

"I had to kill someone for them," Julianna says, but seeing Tui's alarmed reaction adds quickly, "I'm just kidding. I bought them at the Christmas Market."

It's not her fault, she didn't know about Crispin and Moana.

"There's a Christmas Market?" I ask. I wonder why she hasn't told me.

"There was," she confirms, "but I'd say they've gone bonkers with what they were charging for some of the things."

"So, WeFeedU are into growing wheat now?" Tāne wonders.

"They'd be looking at some major climate manipulation facilities for something like that."

"That would explain the huge, converted fields north of the quarry," Enav says. "Didn't look anything like their fake orchards. I wondered what it was that they were growing there. I guess it's that."

"I think the man at the pop-up store was selling stolen grain, if I could judge by his behaviour," I say.

"Stolen?" Tui's ears prick up.

"Stolen groceries are gold mines, nowadays," Enav agreed.

The fickle electricity supply was cut off just as we were sitting at the table. The candles I lit make the table look even better.

"Shall we say a little prayer?" Rāwiri suggests, and I nod with a smile. I'm not particularly religious, but I welcome small gestures, such as giving thanks for the food we have, and for our beloveds.

"I don't believe in God," Tui announces. She's become quite a rebellious fourteen-year-old. I wonder if our past stay with Father Hubbard has anything to do with it.

"You don't have to believe to give thanks," Tāne tells her, more than a little amused.

"Well then, Mr Smarty, if I don't believe in God, who is it that I'm giving thanks to?"

"How about you give thanks to Rāwiri, and to Julianna, who cooked a lovely meal for us?" he suggests, and she reluctantly agrees.

It is almost comical to hear Tui's "Rāwiri and Julianna" mumbled loudly enough over Rāwiri's mention of "Our Lord in Heaven". I'm quite proud of her spirited defiance, but more so I'm grateful for the others not making even the slightest insinuation that they find her annoying.

Tāne helps me serve the food onto plates. He's such a great young man. Now, at twenty-four, he's living on his own, working as a teacher and counsellor at the only school left open in our district. He has no formal qualification, but with so few available teachers still around or living, no qualifications were required, other than, as he put it, 'You were once a child yourself, and you're not completely stupid'. But Tāne was so much more than that. He was kind, compassionate, attentive, and very devoted to his family—his dad, Tui, and me. The way he adopted Tui as his younger sister, even though they were not blood-related, was a testament to his beautiful character, and she, on her part, completely adored him.

Two years ago, when he got this job, he tried to convince me to send Tui to that school, but while I knew he'd be watching closely over her, I couldn't face her being gone for a week at a time, the school being so far away. I was much too fearful for her safety and well-being. In return, I tried to convince Tāne to stay home with us and be Tui's private tutor. But, as he was twenty-two then, and looking forward to establishing himself independently, probably finding a partner at some point, he refused.

"Let's do Christmas presents now!" Tui says.

"Maybe after we eat?" Rāwiri suggests.

"No... please... now?"

Shopping for meaningless mass-produced objects has long

become a consumerist luxury no one could afford. Starting around the Great Famine, shopping centres had closed one after the other, until none survived. On our first Christmas together as a couple, Rāwiri and I decided that each of us would be tasked with writing a nice little poem to someone else. We've been gifting Christmas poems as gifts ever since.

Since no one knew Julianna as well as I did, we rigged the selection, so that she wrote my poem, and I wrote hers. Tui wrote Rāwiri's, Rāwiri Enav's, Enav Tui's, and since everyone was already allocated, and no one was left to write Tāne's, I wrote his as well, and he was given the option to choose whom to write to. He chose Tui. She's been elated by the fact both her brother and her uncle were writing to her.

We each read aloud our poems in turn. They are mostly just a silly attempt to put a smile on each other's faces, not some grand poetic achievements. We giggle at things such as,

'Listen here it's not a fad/ Rāwiri you're the best stepdad/ another year Mum's off the hook/ cause Rāwiri you're a better cook/ you are kind, and you are brave/ but why do you no longer shave?'

"Yeah, what's with the rugged look, Dad?" Tāne asks, and I realise that Rāwiri is smiling, but there's sadness in his eyes. *Maybe it's depression*, I think, and my spirit falls.

"I thought I looked sexy!" Rāwiri says with forced cheer, and the reading party moves on.

'Juniper, you're my best friend through happiness and strife/ but I can't write a good poem to save my life.'

"Nah, that was actually pretty good!" Enav tells Julianna, and everyone agrees.

'Tui, I love you, you're my sister/ and even though you can be as painful as a blister/ you also bring me joy and laughter/ without you Christmas would be a disaster.'

"C'mon! that's a real poor excuse at rhyming. You did better last year!" Tui complains, with a cheeky smile.

"Sorry, I only wrote it half an hour ago... I forgot!" Says Tāne.

"What! You get no strawberries!" Tui says, and we all laugh.

We complete the round of poem reading, and are about to start eating, when Rāwiri says, "Wait, I have one more," and he hands me a poem. "Read it to yourself," he says.

"Oh, not fair!" Tui isn't happy. "Read it aloud Mum!"

"No, no," I say. "This one is mine."

"But it's against the rules!"

"I make the rules," I say and read silently.

'Juniper my love, my star shining bright/ There is no force, no power, no might/ that can make me love you less/ of all the things, you are the best/ You are my soulmate, you are my treasure/ I wish our future in years we could measure/ For my illness I am so sorry/ I hope my end is not too gory/ I didn't wish for this to happen/ but my love for you it sharpened/ If before next Yule I'm gone/ don't be sad, don't be alone/ Our family is now one/ and this should go on when I'm done/ promise me that you'll be fine/ here or not, our love will onwards shine. *From your ever-loving man, Rāwiri.'*

I can sense tears pricking the corners of my eyes. Rāwiri reaches over, grabs my hand in his and kisses it. I fold the paper neatly and place it in my pocket, where Tui's letter already is. Always is. Now I have two.

No one but Rāwiri can sense the turmoil I'm experiencing. They all dig into their food and converse jovially. The thought that he might not be with us next Christmas is too hard to take. Suddenly, I can't eat anything, not even the flatbread, which I was looking forward to eating. I always loved bread so much. Some who lived in The Before missed ice creams and cakes; I just missed simple rye bread. It was the food I craved the most.

"Juniper, have some. I made it for you," Rāwiri says softly.

I force a smile and take a bite. The flavour is incredible. "You outdid yourself, Love," I say, and make myself take another bite.

"How long will you be staying with us, Uncle Enav?" Tui asks.

"Until after New Year," he says, "if that's OK?"

"Of course, it's OK!" Tui and I say in unison.

"They don't mind at the quarry that you're staying away longer?" I ask.

"No, they have some health and safety issues, I think they'd actually prefer fewer workers there at the moment."

"What happened?"

"You haven't heard? They found a body."

Tui's ears perk. "A body?"

"Yes," Enav says and turns to me and Rāwiri. "It's that doctor from the clinic."

"What?" Rāwiri and I are both stunned. "Dr Schubert?"

"Yes, that nice chap from the clinic. He's been murdered."

Suddenly I can't stop my tears anymore. Why is life so unfair? Who would kill such a nice, kind man, who was supporting a starving community? I think about the sick and hungry children who have no one left to feed them now.

"I'm sorry, I didn't know you were close, I didn't mean to bring it up like that," Enav says.

"Do they know who did it?" Rāwiri asks, deeply affected.

"Yes, they have the guy," Enav continues, a bit reluctantly at the sight of my bitter anguish.

"A patient?"

"No. It was a fresh food delivery guy, some go-between for the donors and the clinic. He must have wanted to keep the groceries all to himself and sell them on the black market. A truck full of food can make you rich these days, you know... Anyway, the doctor came outside the clinic to offload the truck, the guy stabbed him in the chest and dropped him in the quarry. He was caught with the truck still parked behind his house," Enav says. "Funny thing is, this doctor, he normally wears a bullet proof vest. It could have saved him, I guess. The one time he left without it, he got murdered."

FIVE YEARS EARLIER: 2048

Twenty

People here, people like me, used to think a famine was something that comes after a long-drawn-out drought. A misfortune that was saved for poor African countries; vast, sun-stricken lands, crumbling under unbearable heat, starved of rainwater, with futile irrigation systems and empty government coffers.

When the Middle East succumbed to a prolonged and fatal lack of water, several years ago, the region sank into an all-out-war. It started with local skirmishes over water resources, and quickly escalated to a cataclysmic collision of countries, armies, and religions. It was a war that had every intention to wipe civilisations out completely. But over here, no one thought we'd be affected by the climate catastrophe in any way that resembled what actually happened.

Sure, temperatures kept rising and rising. Every summer people said it was the hottest one. And every year summer became longer, and hotter.

But we never thought a famine would come after a long-drawn-out rain. The rain that never stopped. Warm sheets of ferocious rain. Hard rain, relentless, angry rain. It drowned whole towns, washed away forests, farmed animals, wildlife, and humans. It completely destroyed farmlands, orchards, wineries, and fields. Within a year, food had become so scarce, prices shot up astronomically, the world economy was in free fall, and society was in collapse.

I can't believe Tui and I managed to get out of the Great Famine alive.

We're now at the tail end of it. I can tell by the fact that fruit and vegetables are more available and somewhat more affordable these days. The human spirit, combined with some ingenuity, had managed to triumph, and find ways to grow food, against the odds.

But the ending of the Great Famine didn't bring relief from the vengeance of the climate; it only meant we could sustain ourselves a little while longer, to face the impact of the damage generations before us had caused.

I wonder what more we'd be forced to handle, as I hold Tui's shaking body in my arms. We're both lying inside the bathtub, as low as we can, while an Armageddon of wind is assaulting us outside, and I know that soon the wind will pick up this house and blow it to smithereens, the bathtub with it, as the cherry on top.

I can't believe our crappy luck. Finally, after all the hardships and tribulations we had to face, finally we moved into this house that was given to us, thinking we'd be safe here. A new start for us, I thought. But I suppose now, as I actually shake in my boots with fear, there is no escaping the wrath of nature, not in the old house, not in this house, not anywhere.

The wind is so loud, I can't hear my own screams. I'm grateful not to be able to hear Tui's screams either, because that would have broken my heart. She's holding Rufus, her old teddy bear, in her arms, and I bet he's screaming too.

I really liked this house. Even though we hadn't lived in it long enough to embed ourselves in its features, to imprint fresh new memories within its walls, it had so much promise. It sat clear above sea level and away from the flood zones, a small patch where I thought I could put a playhouse for Tui, and maybe try to plant something, whatever might grow. It was a small house, but sturdy and clean, no mud marking the solid walls. Two small bedrooms for us, even though since living in the old house, and especially following that night when Crispin and Moana were murdered, Tui slept with me in my bed; I knew, however, that at some point she'd grow out of it and seek her privacy.

So, while small, there was room to grow here. I even liked the windowless bathroom, the cocooning of it, the privacy. I didn't mind it not having a window. Now, spooning Tui amid these pale green walls, inside this old, cast-iron tub, I know it's only a matter of minutes before the walls give in.

"I love you!" I shout as hard as I can, not sure if Tui can hear me.

The sound of the walls cracking is terrifying. The roof is about to give. I lock my arms as tight as I can. *Don't snatch this girl away from me! Don't you dare! Take me. Only me.*

With every further second we're still alive, I grow more aware of my body, and realise I'm crying. *Please, please, please, please let us get out of this alive.*

Pieces of the roof disappear, ripped by a ferocious hand and thrown away, now the wind is in the house, it has penetrated our space, wreaking havoc in its wake. The walls are shaking, the floorboards rattle so hard, I briefly remember those joyrides I used to love as a child, at the carnival, the teacups that would spin and spin around and around, leaving your heart in your mouth.

I can hear the destruction, but I'm not sure where it is. I close my eyes tight, Tui still in my arms.

I love you; I love you; I love you; I love you!

I keep saying to her in my head. There is the smell of seawater, shaved wood, and powdered concrete in the air. I feel soil thrown onto my face. For a moment the noise is so hard, I feel I might faint. My body is so stiff, I'm just another plank of wood for the wind to strip and throw away. But then, all falls silent.

Twenty One

We rise from the wreckage as two ghosts. Nothing is left in one piece, other than the bathtub and a couple of inner walls. Around us is a sea of debris, broken pieces of the life that was. With the years, this place had known more and more tornados, more and more frequently, but I had never known a tornado to leave such destruction behind it. In terms of the vast diameter of this complete chaos, there had never been anything like it.

Tui is in shock. This nine-year-old child had already lived through so much trauma. I take her hand in mine, and we step away from the skeleton of the place where I hoped we could live for years to come. I check my pocket, Tui's letter is there, so is the money I grabbed from the safe when the storm appeared. It's the only money we had left, and we needed it to survive. I pick up a kitchen knife I see on the ground and shove it under my belt. Some protection, at least.

"Where are we going, Mummy?" Tui asks.

I look around. In The Before, when a disaster struck and communities were faced with adverse reactions, there was always spontaneous help to spring up from compassionate members of society. Soup kitchens would have been erected, schools would open their gymnasiums to shelter the refugees, some welfare support would have been provided. But now, whoever survived—the Great Famine, the floods, the rising sea water, the loss of livelihood, the destruction, poverty, and loss—was not interested in anyone else's problems. The very structure of society was crumbling.

"I don't know, sweetheart," I answer.

I really don't know. But we have to get away from here before darkness. Darkness compounds real, life-threatening danger, on top of any adversity. I try to imagine where the dusty road once was and start walking in that direction. If I'm right, we must be going north, and sooner or later will find traces of communities, or whatever was left.

Here and there, in the periphery, there are a few survivors like us. Most of them seem to be looking around, searching. None seems to be walking away. As we pass through wreckage, we come to see a woman sitting on the ground, crying. She seems to be lost and confused. We may be walking through what was once her house.

"Are you OK? Can I help you?" I ask her. I don't know what I can do, or what help I could possibly offer, but I can't just ignore her and walk away.

She's on the ground, her eyes wide open with shock. "What happened?" she asks, and repeats, "What happened?"

"There was a tornado, I believe. A great big one," I answer. "We lost our house," I say and point to where the skeletal remains of two inner walls and one massive bathtub still stand. "That was our house, there."

She follows my finger and nods, still unable to connect the dots. She must be in her mid-twenties, her short, bronze-red hair, frizzed like a crown of twigs.

"We're going to look for shelter," I say. "It's not safe to stay here, outside, in the dark."

She looks at me but doesn't appear to acknowledge what I say.

I reach out my free hand, "Let me help you up."

She grabs my hand and lifts herself up from the ground, looking around, taking in the destruction.

At once, she turns her head back to me and asks, "have you seen Sammy?"

"We haven't seen anyone, other than you, since the storm," I say. "Who is Sammy?" I ask, dreading the answer.

"My son. My little boy, he's only four," she says and her voice cracks with the bitter devastation of finally coming to terms with what might have happened. "Sammy!" she cries, "Sammy!"

"Sammy!" I join her. Not that for a moment I believe Sammy will be found, but I had to. What sort of people were we if we didn't help each other in such times? "Sammy!"

We walk around, calling "Sammy!" Tui joins us. Sammy isn't found. He could have been thrown miles and miles in the air. It could be days before any of the people who were lost here will be found, if ever.

After futile calls for Sammy, I feel we really must be going.

"We need to leave here," I say to the woman. "You should come with us. It isn't safe here now."

The woman crouches and sits herself back on the ground. "I can't leave. What if Sammy comes home when I'm away?"

I watch her. Does she really not understand what happened? She turns her head away from us, and just sits there. My heart sinks. I realise that I would have done the exact same thing. If Tui was lost in the storm, I'd wait until the end of time for her to come back.

Twenty Two

We must've been walking a good three hours without stopping or resting, and still we haven't reached any sign of civilisation. On the way we see smashed cars, bits of roofs and other debris, tossed away like toys. In the corner of my eye, I can identify scattered bodies as we went. Thrown like ragged dolls, faceless. I decide not to look. The last thing I want is to see a lifeless red-headed boy named Sammy. I dread it. I had a fair idea of what a four-year-old dead child looked like. Memories of Moana's bloodied body on the floor nearly cause me to stumble. I mustn't think about it. Not now.

Tui has been so good until now, not complaining once as we kept marching on, but is showing signs of struggle. We slow down considerably.

"My feet really hurt, Mummy."

"I know, sweetheart. You've been so brave so far."

Every cell in my body is aching to keep on going, but I can't break Tui, she needs a rest. "Let's catch our breaths, eh?"

The ground is wet and muddy, but there are old dry stumps of fallen trees scattered around. Tui sits, Rufus the bear in her hands, as

I look for wild wood sorrels, those with the juicy long stems that are good enough to eat. I pick up a bunch, and we sit together and munch through them. Tui leans her head against my shoulder.

"I love you," I whisper to her soft hair.

"I love you too."

I allow her just a few more minutes to rest before I spring to my feet. "Time to get going again, sweetheart."

"Can't we rest here a little bit longer?"

"No, Tui. I'm sorry. The ground here is soft, if heavy rain starts soon, not only do we risk getting completely drenched, but mud slips become a real hazard."

Reluctantly she gets up and slowly, we start walking again. Half an hour later, the rain starts.

*

Finally, there are small houses ahead. Few and far between, most seem to be deserted. Gaping holes where windows once were, rotten weatherboards for cladding. I'm so disoriented, I'm not exactly sure where we are. There are plenty of small communities, villages, and sleepy towns that had grown more and more deserted as the climate catastrophe worsened. The charge of rising seas and perpetual, violent floods, the deadly slips and giant tornados, the Great Famine—these were only part of it. One of the impacts no one had foreseen was the disease brought by rotting animals.

For well over a decade, climate activists were trying to convince governments, industries, and individuals to change to plant-based economies as the only way out of an apocalypse, but only a few had listened. By the time governments were frantically trying to impose change, it was already years too late.

Initially, changes in the climate had crept in stealth mode, slowly and steadily, increasing slightly, year by year. After a while, however, change came roaring, and panic-stricken people were finally listening. Agriculture, as a sector, was slowly being abandoned, but the animals who were forcefully bred only to be exploited and consumed as pieces of dead flesh, were not about to see a happily-ever-after. Some were urgently slaughtered and shipped overseas to countries that were slower to shift. Some were consumed locally by people who remained defiant. Some were killed on abandoned farms, the more fortunate ones by a bullet to their head, but as life regressed further, many were drowned, sledgehammered, or clubbed to death. Within twelve months, thousands were left to rot in the relentless rain. As the Great Famine intensified, however, some desperate people took to seeking out the carcasses and using whatever was still salvageable. Human consumption of the rotting flesh brought new kinds of zoonotic diseases no one knew before. The population dwindled, and what was left was unrecognisable as the friendly, supportive society that was there before.

*

It's raining hard by the time we approach the old village. I grab Tui's hand in mine as we walk between the derelict buildings. It's clear some of the ruins are inhabited; here, a few clothes on a washing line, there, some plates, and cups in a pile, ready to be washed in the rain-water collection-pots outside. But I can observe no people. There are no curious faces in windows; no one comes out to check who the passing, strange woman and child are. It's quite eerie. I get an ominous feeling in my gut, but don't quite know what to base it on.

"Mummy, I'm so tired," Tui says. I can sense her exhaustion by the way she leans into my hand.

I stop to look around, and she keeps walking, bumping into me, absent-mindedly. I don't think we could go on much further. Night is fast approaching, and the rain might not cease all night. I dread the thought of staying here, but it seems like there is no other choice.

I survey the houses that do not look occupied. One of them still has most of its roof. I drag Tui towards it.

"We might need to stay here tonight, Tui," I say.

She nods lethargically.

I bet it used to be a pretty little house, with its weatherboards painted white and flowerbeds in the front garden. I bet there was a homeowner who was proud of this little house; maybe a cat or a dog lived here once too, sunbathing on the windowsill, succumbing to the caress of the afternoon sun.

I step inside. It is damp and fairly dark. The walls are bare now, and some of the floorboards are missing. What floor remains is covered with debris. From the way what's left of the rooms is set up, it looks like an old-style cottage. No open plan, wide kitchen-diner here. A couple of old kitchen chairs have remained, albeit broken. I walk between the rooms and walk between them again. I don't notice any signs of life here. There isn't a single mattress, a single cup, or a plate. Still, something niggles inside me.

I choose a corner of what must have been a bedroom, still covered with a roof, and with its floorboards intact. We won't be conspicuous here. I train my eyes to follow and memorise the shortest route from the corner to the front door in case we need to evacuate.

"Here, sweetheart," I tell Tui. "Come, you can lie down here, on the floor."

She waits for no further invitation and drops. I position myself next to Tui, leaning against the wall, so that she can rest her head on my left thigh. She falls asleep almost immediately, hugging Rufus. I reach my hand into my pocket and feel inside. Tui's letter and the money, it's all still there. I sigh with some relief and grab the kitchen knife in my right hand, staring into the growing darkness. I don't want to fall asleep.

Twenty Three

I stare into the darkness. Sleep has become a luxury since that night, three years ago. My ears are alert to any sound outside, any footsteps, but so far, there is only intermittent rain, and the sound of my stomach. In the stillness, it starts protesting hunger with loud gargles that echo noisily like an old boat motor.

The past eight years have taught me to settle for little food. Whatever I could grow, forage, or buy, I'd give most of it to Tui. She was growing tall and strong, and in those times, when thousands were dying for lack of food, shelter, or medicine, or falling victim to human cruelty, having her looking relatively healthy and well fed was an enormous achievement, but an equally enormous task. My foraging skills are very good, but the wrath of the climate changes the flora so frequently, I feel I'm always on the back foot with finding wild berries, nettles, fruit, and edible leaves.

She stirs a little but is still asleep. It's truly a wonder how she can sleep so soundly, so easily, pretty much anywhere and in any conditions. She was always an easy child. Maybe because she was my fate. Tui was born one year before the official start of the Great Famine. Of course, things were already bad, but we didn't expect them to get so much worse. I was worried when I was pregnant with her, and yet, I was confident all would be well. I knew she'd come; I was waiting for her. But with Moana, it was a different story.

The hair on my arms stands on end when my thoughts take me to Moana. I know I'm trespassing on my own rules, not to think about it. Push it back, bury it. I can't help it.

I should have been more careful. The impact of famine was already felt that night when Crispin and I weren't careful enough. It wasn't named 'The Great Famine' back then, that's the term people started to use only a couple of years ago, when the full horror of what took place was revealed. Food, however, was becoming very scarce, and whatever there was, was daily getting more expensive.

Crispin was still teaching at the local school; every day he'd come home reporting fewer and fewer students showing up. We'd only just managed to clean the house of the muddy water that flooded it, again, and restore some liveability to it. Tui was sixteen months old, an easy-going, happy baby, who I refused to leave for even a moment, certainly not in the care of strangers. I gave up my secretary job at the accounting company to be her full-time mother. Things had become tense between Crispin and me. Money was becoming short, the repeated floods weren't helping, and my refusal to find Tui a nanny or place her in a day-care facility was becoming more and more of a delicate conversation as the days passed, and the international economy collapsed. But we managed. I planted a wide range of vegetables in raised garden beds at the back of the house and tended to the fruit trees that were showing signs of duress. I managed to save the apple, the avocado, and the feijoa trees, but the mango and plum were lost. We weren't starving, so maybe we didn't quite realise how desperate the situation was growing, I'm not sure what drove us to be so careless that night.

When I think about it, I can suddenly recall the scent of Crispin's skin. It's as if he's right there with me again, with his dark hair and green eyes, his disproportionally wide shoulders and neck that he used to credit to his college rugby days, his full lips…

We met at university, before I dropped out. He was my first true love, my rock in stormy waters. Orphaned and desperate for a home, I was only twenty-two when we wed. We were in no rush to have children. He started teaching, and I, not wanting or able to fund academic studies anymore, had completed a short course at the polytechnic, and got a job as a secretary at a large and well-known accounting company. My pay was average, working hours were decent; I came home on time to cook dinner for Crispin and me and our nights were full of careful passion—everything seemed to be so positive. I was happy. When I found I was pregnant with Tui, three years later, I knew it was fate. But Moana…

I gently strike Tui's hair, her head heavy on my thigh. I remember that day Crispin and I had a terrible fight. He was worried he might lose his job as a teacher, accusing me of being selfish not to be looking for a job.

"You can't be serious!" I remember shouting, "What do you think I'm doing all day if not a job? I'm a mother, that's my job!"

"We need a bigger income, Juniper, what's so hard to understand here?" he shouted back, the vein at the side of his enormous neck visibly pulsing.

"To do what with? Pay a nanny? Where's the logic in that?"

"I told you, my cousin could look after Tui."

"Oh, for heaven's sake, she's thirteen! I'm not leaving Tui with a thirteen-year-old, are you out of your mind?"

"She's a good kid!"

"That's not the point!"

"What is the point then? Don't you understand, we'll soon be forced out of this house?"

"What do you mean? Why is that?"

He paused and took a deep breath before saying, "I haven't been paid by the school."

That threw me. "How come?"

"Mrs Swindon died in the floods, as well as Mrs Connors, the assistant, and they haven't found someone to do the accounts yet."

"I thought it was all automated."

"No, not for a year or so now; not since the support company sank, with the civil war that's still going on in America."

"Shit."

"Yeah."

"How long since you weren't paid, Crispin?"

"Six weeks," he said finally, ashamed.

"Six weeks?" I shuddered. "How come you haven't told me?"

"I don't know. I didn't want to worry you. Every day they say it's going to be sorted."

I shook my head. The sky was falling over us, so fast, so loudly, so completely. Tui was awakened by our shouting. I picked her up from the crib, she was warm and smelled so sweet, like a cinnamon bun. I could still remember cinnamon buns. Cuddled in my arms she immediately calmed, resting her head on my shoulder.

"I can help. I can tidy up the accounts," I threw the offer into the air before I could fully consider it. "But only if I can bring Tui with me. No babysitter, no cousin."

His eyes lit, and a relieved smile brightened his handsome face. "I'm pretty sure that's what they call win-win," he said as he hugged me, Tui still in my arms.

I'm fairly convinced that was the night we had the sex that led to my pregnancy with Moana. Too deeply enthralled in hopes that everything was going to be fine, too eager to see life as a promise and not a disaster, too unprotected, too careless, too stupid.

My Mum had always told me that her pregnancy with me was easier than the one with Enav, because a second baby is always easier to carry and deliver. But it was totally different for me. Maybe because Tui was always meant to be, and Moana was unplanned, a surprise I wasn't ready for, the fruit of a night of unguarded passion.

Carrying her was difficult. I swelled early, my ankles ballooned, my breath shortened. That summer the apple tree hardly had any fruit at all, and some of the vegetables rotted in the soil. I needed to 'eat for two' but with obsessively trying to feed Tui enough, I was eating for less than one. I was so hungry all the time, it drove me near mad. I had to stop helping at the school, and again tension at home grew. I was so stressed all the time; bile was burning my oesophagus day and night. The only good thing in my life was Tui. She was two and she was thriving. I kept going back to the letter I had written her all those years ago, folded carefully in the top drawer with my underwear. Something about it still being there, still kept, instilled calm and reassurance.

It's no wonder that when Moana was born, she was four weeks early, and small for a baby her age. Crispin ran out of the house, that night when the pain started, and woke the midwife who lived down the street, by banging on her door. She came in, still in her nightgown and robes. The pain was excruciating, but it only took Moana a couple of hours before I was able to push her out, screaming.

"She's a delicate one, this one," the midwife neighbour said.

She wrapped her in some towels and placed her at my breast. I remember holding her, her creased face red, her toothless mouth trying to latch at my nipple. She was so small.

Crispin was exceptionally tender and loving the weeks after Moana was born. He took a second night job at the District Disaster Response Centre, helping to fill bags with sand and delivering them where they were needed, clearing flooded houses, and rescuing stranded people with the aid of life jackets and kayaks. It wasn't paying much but it helped ease the growing burden, a little.

Moana was constantly sick. Her growth was stunted, and her motor development wasn't a straight line up. I loved her, of course I loved her, but she drained me. It wasn't the same as it was with Tui; love wasn't instant but slow to grow, and I constantly berated and blamed myself for comparing them.

"I'm hungry, Mummy," Tui would say, and my heart broke into little pieces.

The method for rationing our food had to shift. In order to remain lactating for Moana, I had to eat more, and that meant cutting down Tui's portions. I hated myself for having to do that. It went against every maternal instinct I had. I tried not to blame Moana for it, but it was so hard, it was just so hard. But it was the raiding of the back garden that broke me. Thieves broke through the gate and stole all the vegetables that I so carefully grew there. Disrespectful, vile hands, picked, dug, and took everything, leaving the soil turned, empty, riddled with gaping holes, like mouths begging to be fed, like my children's mouths.

Crispin returned that night to find me on the floor. So deep in my despair, so withdrawn, I couldn't hear Moana's screams in her crib, or feel Tui's little hand stroking my hair so gently. He picked me up, put me in bed next to Tui, picked up Moana and left. I didn't know where. I didn't ask. I'm not sure I cared. When they finally returned, he had a bag of food with him, full of fruit and vegetables, and some beans and seeds. His eyes didn't meet mine, as he placed the bag on the kitchen table. I didn't ask where he got it, I didn't want to know. In my heart I assumed the worst, and I didn't blame him. We've become those people. People who'd do anything to feed their children. Anything.

Anything.

Twenty Four

When Moana was two, still small and underdeveloped, the floods returned. The rain just didn't stop. For days on end, it poured nonstop, occasionally with the additional thunderstorm. After three days the river broke, and we knew our time in that house was nearly up. This time it was clear that no pile of sandbags was going to save us. A couple of escape bags had been ready waiting by the door for some time, and still, it was so hard to leave. We had nowhere to go. By the time we evacuated, water was already knee-high inside the house, and by the state of things, we would have drowned within two hours had we stayed. With Tui on Crispin's shoulders and Moana in my arms, Tui's letter safely in my pocket, and two small bags, we left the house that had been our home since our marriage.

Our first stop was the District Disaster Response Centre; that was still safe from the floods back then.

"Maybe they could help us,' Crispin said. "Houses clear all the time, not all of them because of diseases, so maybe they can direct us somewhere."

Inhabiting a deserted house was not an idea that appealed to me at all, but we needed a roof over our heads, and the options were incredibly narrow.

"Crispin!" a middle-aged man with bushy hair and thick stubble welcomed us. "Thank goodness you're all safe."

He walked us into the office and offered us some tea, and biscuits that tasted like they'd expired a year earlier. Still, we wolfed them down, picking crumbs with our fingers.

"I managed to find something for you, Crispin," the man said as he returned. "Not the best area, but the house is dry and partially furnished."

He seemed like he wanted to say something more but wasn't sure. Looking at me, words seemed to get stuck in his mouth.

"Erm, it, uh, it used to, erm, belong to, the house, I mean, it used to belong to one of our staff," he coughed, and rubbed his square chin, his entire body language screaming discomfort. 'She, uh, she, erm, she died. She died."

"What happened to her?" I asked.

"Beg your pardon?"

"What happened to her?"

"She uh, well, of what we know, yeah, she was, erm, murdered."

"In the house?"

"Um, yes, yes."

I looked at Crispin with great disdain.

"Beggars can't be choosers, Juniper," he said, and I knew he was right.

It was nearly dark by the time the man dropped us at the empty house, which was now our own. I understood what he meant by it not being in the best area. At the best of times, in The Before, this neighbourhood was a neglected, crime-riddled part of town, but now it really looked like a menacing slum. The way we were watched by people as we stood at the door made me shudder.

"It's only for a little while," Crispin whispered as he pushed open the door, "until we can stand on our own two feet again."

Surprisingly, the inside of the house was nice. Small, but pleasant. The front door opened to the small kitchen that also served as a dining room, with a short hall to a backdoor. All the windows were hung with deep blue curtains; only the front kitchen window included another layer of some old-fashioned lacey needlework underneath. A single bedroom that we had to all share, a smaller, doorless, sitting room next to it, a tiny bathroom with a toilet that still worked, and a narrow, green tub were all there was. It was clean, with the white walls and the tidy kitchen, and a round dining table in the middle.

We put the girls to sleep on the mattress on the floor, while Crispin and I squeezed together on the king-single bed. In the morning, our backs and necks stiff and hurting, it was clear that these sleeping arrangements had to be reconsidered. From then on, Tui slept with me on the bed and Crispin was on the floor with Moana.

While indoors the house was cosy and homey, outside seemed hostile. When we arrived, there were burned car carcasses decorating the roads, and every day there seemed to be more of them. We could hear windows being smashed, frequent loud shouts between groups of men, occasionally gun fire.

It felt as if we were always watched. Always observed. The first morning, when Crispin left us to go to school, I locked the front door behind him, then rushed to the back door to secure it as well. Around midday, while trying to nap through pangs of hunger, I swore I awoke from the rattle of the front door. Someone was trying to get in. I froze, my hand on Tui. After a while all went quiet again. I rushed to the living room and drew all the curtains shut. Day or night, we were now shrouded in darkness.

Living shut out from the world, with no fresh air or natural light, would affect even the strongest of persons. And I was far from being the strongest of persons.

At first, the District Disaster Response Centre provided us with a bit of food every week. It wasn't much, but it helped us greatly. Slowly, the food parcels became smaller, and seemed to grow increasingly eclectic, with mixed cans and bags of expired grains, that seemed to be put together out of whatever could be rummaged from dead people's pantries. Tui rarely complained of being hungry, but ever since she'd been weaned off my breastmilk, Moana cried almost constantly. She was nearly three now, and still small, wobbly on her feet, and hardly speaking. I didn't know where to take her to be seen, to be diagnosed. Clinics were closing down, hospitals were overflowing. In a sea of hungry, underdeveloped children, no one would pay attention to yet another hungry, underdeveloped child. I felt so desperate, and so alone. So very alone.

There was only Tui.

The more Moana grew irritable and demanding, Tui showed herself to be content and comfortable. At only five, she tried to help me with Moana, entertaining her little sister with songs and games, drawing her attention away from food and hunger. I don't know what I would've done without her.

In the many hours we had to pass in the locked house, the happiest were those spent teaching Tui to read and write. She picked it up so quickly, it filled me with so much pride. I could almost see her brain as it expanded. In no time, she had developed a love of books. Now, whenever Crispin went foraging, he tried to find some books for her to read. Her shrieks of joy as she saw the promising rectangle surprise in his hand, were the greatest reward. I'd watch her read, sitting on the bed, entirely engrossed in the story, flying with witches, battling with dragons, or adventuring with wild wolves, and I'd wonder, who was the child this book belonged to before? What happened to them? But I dared not ask.

And still, every few days, the front door rattled, and I'd freak out. Crispin would come home from a very long day, to find me at the end of my tether, barely functioning.

"We can't stay here, Crispin," I cried on one such occasion. "Someone or some people are constantly trying to break in through the front door."

Crispin was clearly worried but didn't know what to do about it.

"Where will we go, Juniper?"

"People are dropping like flies, surely there are houses emptying in better areas."

"The better areas are all flooded,' he said. 'This place is becoming a ghost town. I don't think the school will remain open for very much longer either."

"What will we do?"

"I don't know."

"We have to leave."

"I already explained it, Juniper, there's nowhere to go."

"I can't stay here alone with the girls every day, Crispin. Not with the door being tested like that," my voice was shaking. "One day they'll break it, or break the window, and they'll get inside. They'll kill us." I took a deep breath, "And anyway, I thought about it. We can move to live with my brother Enav. He lives up north. He'll help us."

"When was the last time you spoke to Enav? Do you even know where he is?"

"North."

"North. Where north?"

I wasn't sure. Last time I had seen him was before Moana was born. He said he'd met a nice girl, and he was planning to move in with her, maybe have a child together. I couldn't recall the name of the place, or the girl. My brain had turned to mush.

"Listen, I have an idea," Crispin said. "Let's get a dog. A big guard dog, to scare people away. He can stay inside the house with you and keep you company."

"Another mouth to feed?" I asked, sincerely surprised by the illogical proposition.

"I'm pretty sure canned dog food is still easier to find than human canned food," Crispin replied.

I didn't know where he had the confidence to come up with such a statement. Even as he said it, it sounded absurd. I'm sure starving humans would eat canned dog food without hesitation if they had to.

"We have canned dog food at the District Disaster Relief Centre," he added. "And, if some people threaten the house, or you and the girls, the dog could attack them and eat them. Problem solved."

I looked at Crispin unamused, trying to figure out if he was serious or joking.

"I believe they call it a win-win," he said.

"He would eat the other people, but not us?" I asked, baffled by his skewed logic. In what world was that a win-win?

"I was only joking, Juniper."

I wanted to believe him.

I wouldn't have minded a dog in the house with us. I missed Johnny. I missed having an animal companion. Animals were always true, always there, always trusting. Offering unconditional love, no matter what. But getting a dog to look after us, with not enough food to feed ourselves, was madness.

"Let's go to the dog pound on Saturday," Crispin suggested. "With so many people dead, there are bound to be dozens of dogs without owners, begging to find a good new home."

What had gotten into him? Was it he who was suddenly so desperate for a dog companion? He sounded serious, even excited. The whole thing was outrageously stupid. I worried Crispin had been driven mad by the way our lives had deteriorated.

"What's going on, Mummy?" Tui asked, sensing the shift in the atmosphere at home.

"We're going to get a dog," I said, and couldn't help but smile.

Maybe I had gone half-mad too.

Twenty Five

What I first noticed, as we approached the pound, was the silence. Normally you'd hear barking long before you'd even see the yellow sign on the lamppost, at the crossroads, directing you to the kennels. One dog would start, and then they'd set each other off, and the deafening choir of barks would carry for miles. But there was nothing, only the still hush that was, in itself, deafening.

We approached the kennels, Tui's hand in mine, Moana on Crispin's shoulders. The high meshed fences towered above us; some old plastic sheets blew in the light wind. The place seemed to be deserted and felt eerie and foreboding. A weird smell wafted about the place; flies hovered above us as we walked closer. I snuck a worried look at Crispin, who seemed to be as clueless as I was.

"Where are the dogs, Mummy?" Tui asked.

I hushed her. We shouldn't be announcing ourselves.

The pound office was just a small cabin at the front of the kennels. The glass door was open. There was even a sign on it that said 'OPEN'. Crispin stepped forward, ahead of Tui and me.

A woman in khaki uniform sat on a manager's chair inside. When she saw us, she rose and came to meet us at the door. The words 'POUND STAFF' were embroidered into her khaki uniform, and the name tag 'Carol' was pinned above her left breast.

"Yes?" she said, before we even had the chance to say hello. No one said hello anymore.

"We're here for a dog," Crispin said.

"OK. How much?" the woman asked, very matter-of-factly.

The question seemed out of place. What did she mean by *'how much'*? How much we were willing to pay? I thought it was going to be free of charge, rescuing a lonely shelter dog in times like these. I wasn't planning on paying anything.

"Pardon?" Crispin asked.

"How much?" the woman repeated the question, making us none the wiser. Seeing that we weren't answering, she continued, "We have them in one, three or five kilos. All mixed breeds so I can't guarantee quality, but they're fresh."

I thought I understood, as my stomach was turning. By the look on his face, Crispin had figured it out too.

"Oh, no, sorry, we were looking for an actual dog, you know. A dog. A living, breathing dog."

The woman, Carol, burst into a short, loud, snort.

"A living dog?" she cackled, "What, is it twenty-forty still?" She cleared her throat. "Sir, look around you. There are no dogs, no cats, no animals. People are eating their own pets. I bet they'll be eating their own kids too, soon enough," she looked at Moana as she said it.

I felt dizzy. Where were we living? *Under a rock, that's where.* Shut behind drawn curtains, behind locked doors, supplied with a small parcel from the District Disaster Response Centre every week. I really didn't see how bad the famine was growing all around us. We were having it easy compared to so many.

"So, there are no dogs?" Crispin asked, still digesting the information.

"The dogs are for eating, Sir."

Tui started crying, triggering Moana who started crying too.

I'm not sure what made us so shocked. Animals were killed to be eaten for centuries. What made dogs less 'for eating' than pigs, cows, or sheep? I bet the nameless cow who was taken to be slaughtered was just as terrified, just as confused by the betrayal of the humans, and valued her life just as much as Timmy the spaniel.

We turned and walked away from there as fast as we could.

Twenty Six

It wasn't long after that the school was closed down. Only a handful of children were still coming every day, most likely due to the kind principal who tried her best to feed them, out of her own pantry. Now the four of us were stuck in the small house, all of us hungry, agitated, aimless. The District Disaster Response Centre was still open, but completely overwhelmed. After all, the entire country, indeed the entire world, was experiencing a single, prolonged, deep, overwhelming catastrophe. Which to respond to first?

Food supplies dwindled steadily, until there was none left. Dead people's houses were raided as soon as the person breathed their last, but more often than not, only to find empty pantries there too.

Hunger is a weird thing. If you train your mind, you can almost get over it. After going without for very long, you can push it so far back in your mind, that you might almost forget you're hungry. But it can also work the other way, take over your mind, and drive you to the limits of your sanity. It seemed in our house, two of us managed to live with the constant hunger, and two of us struggled to the point of breaking.

Crispin and Moana were the weaker link. It drove Crispin to leave us every night and look for food. He'd stay out until the early hours of the morning, sometimes only returning mid-morning, banging on the door, 'Juniper! It's me, open up!' At times, he came back holding some vegetables that were clearly stolen from someone's garden, at times cans of beans or pasta that expired months earlier; at times he came back empty-handed.

I would lie in bed, and in my heart, I knew we were not going to survive this. There was no way.

And then, it happened.

Moana had just turned four, looking frail and small. We celebrated her birthday with a tiny portion of beans that Crispin brought that morning. We were sitting at the round kitchen table, singing 'Happy Birthday' when the front door burst open in a loud crash.

A man was standing there, holding a huge, pointed knife that looked fiercely sharp. His eyes were dark, hidden under a thick shock of hair, and the air about him was deeply menacing. The four of us jumped out of our seats. I grabbed Tui, who was seated right next to me, and took a few steps backwards, towards the hall that led to the backdoor.

"Moana, come to Mummy!" I called to her, reaching out my other hand, but the man shouted, "Don't move, girl!"

Moana froze.

Crispin, who was closer to her, grabbed Moana's hand, and pushed her behind him.

Come to me, come to me, come to me, come to me.

Moana didn't move.

"We don't have any food, only these beans," Crispin, who stood nearest to the man, said. "Take them, here, take them, and leave."

"Don't move!" the man shouted again, now bringing the knife forward.

I tightened my grip on Tui, taking another step backwards. Tui and I were now a couple of steps into the hall. I still had clear sight of the kitchen, but Tui, who I pushed slightly behind me, was out of the man's sight.

"Run and unlock the backdoor, Tui. Now!" I whispered to her, trying not to move my facial muscles, as if I were a ventriloquist.

Tui, so smart and resilient for her six years of age, obeyed immediately.

"Take the food, man. We don't have any more than what you see on the table," Crispin repeated.

I could hear Tui unlocking the backdoor.

"Moana, come to me," I called to her again.

"I said don't move!" the man shouted, and took a deep, long look at Moana.

In a terrible instant I finally realised. The man wasn't there for our food. *We* were the food.

I played the next few seconds in my mind over and over, night after night since. Everything happened in an instant. The man leaped forward, slicing Crispin's neck, then Moana's. I watched Moana fall down to the floor, her blood spraying over the table, the wall.

I remember, in almost slow motion, Tui behind me shouting "Mummy! It's open!" and I remember, painfully, turning around and running to the back door, grabbing Tui, and leaping over the few steps onto the yard, then running into the road. I recall looking back at the house, knowing what was taking place inside, then running. A manic run, a hysterical run, Tui with me; we ran, and we ran, until I couldn't feel my lungs or my feet.

It was dark. I didn't know where we were. There were no more houses, no burned car carcasses, no people. Rain started falling. I hugged Tui to me, tears rolling down my face. I didn't know what to say. I didn't know what to do.

"I love you," I said finally.

"I love you too, Mummy," she said.

Then, after a small pause, she asked, her voice sweet and full of worry.

"What happened to Daddy and Moana?"

Yes, what happened? What's just happened?

My hands were shaking, and my head was spinning. *What's just happened?* I was gripped by deep, overwhelming shock. I wasn't sure what to say. What had just happened to us didn't seem real. *Did it really happen?* Yes, it did.

"They're gone, my love. They're gone. They're gone. Gone. Gone..." I burst into tears, hugging Tui tightly. They were gone. Gone. Gone. Gone. No matter how many times I repeated the thought, it wouldn't register. *They're gone.*

Suddenly, a thought had frozen me. I reached into my pocket and cold sweat dripped down my back. The letter! It wasn't there!

"Oh, no!" I said. "No, no, no, no, no, no!"

"What happened, Mummy?" Tui looked at me, worried.

"There is a letter, I left it in the house!" I said, frustrated at my own stupidity.

"What letter?"

"It's a letter I'd written when I was nine years old. It means a lot to me, Tui. This letter, it's… it's almost like my fate, your fate… it's hard to explain."

"Where is it?"

"In the underwear drawer. I left it in the house." *Stupid. Stupid!*

"What are we going to do?"

I felt so confused, so overwhelmed. It was a complete insanity to go back now. We made it; we were safe. I couldn't believe that even in light of what's just happened to us, all I could worry about was the stupid letter. *They're gone. Gone!*

I must get the letter back!

I must get the letter!

They're gone. Gone. Gone. Murdered. Eaten.

I must get the letter!

"Can't you write another letter?" Tui asked.

I smiled a sad smile and shook my head. I must have lost my mind. Was it the shock? Maybe. Temporary insanity perhaps. A burden of grief that I wasn't able to manage. Maybe. But in my heart, I already knew that I had to go back to retrieve the letter. Mad as it was. I'd had it for so long. I'd had it from before Tui was even a possibility. I just knew she'd come. I'd written it for her. This letter had some strange power, I truly believed it. I didn't think for a moment that I was only imagining it. I sensed it deeply. It was almost paranormal the way it defined my life. In a way that I was willing to admit was nearly absurd, I believed the letter kept Tui safe. I had to get it back.

Twenty Seven

We walked back in the darkness and the rain, away from the road, hiding in shadows. When we finally reached the neighbourhood, I walked Tui further away from the road, until we reached a small, evergreen tree. I helped her climb to the lower branches.

"Wait for me here. If I'm not back by first light, run."

Why was I risking her, and myself for the letter? I kept asking myself, but I couldn't answer. I felt an irrational pull, compelling me to go back and take it. Sneaking through people's backyards, crouching behind old, broken, wheelbarrows and empty garden sheds, I finally reached the house. I jumped over the low fence, into the backyard. The backdoor was open, the way we had left it. Stealthily, I moved closer. No sound was coming from the inside. I picked a stone and tossed it in through the door, ready to start running, but nothing happened. The house was still.

One small step after another, I walked in.

The short hall opened to the kitchen. It was now deserted. I stifled a cry with my hand, seeing the floor covered in a pool of blood, with a thick trail of it leading all the way through the front door, and out. *They're gone. Gone. Gone. Murdered. Eaten! They're being eaten right now! Right outside! My baby girl! Moana… Crispin…*

Everything was beyond surreal. The beans we ate together only a few hours before, were still on the table. My head felt foggy and heavy. In some way, I knew that I came back not only to retrieve the letter, but also to make sure the whole thing really happened. That I wasn't hallucinating or dreaming. But now that I was there, even though I knew it truly did happen, it still seemed impossible.

Tears blinded me. What was I doing back in the house, risking myself and Tui so carelessly? *Get the letter.* I had to move fast, before someone might have spotted me through the open front door. I ran to the drawer, grabbed the letter, and placed it in my pocket. Just as I was about to sneak out again, I noticed Rufus on the bed. Tui's beloved teddy bear. I grabbed him and ran.

Out through the back door, over the fence, through backyards, out into the road.

They were standing there, about a hundred meters away, over an open fire. Maybe five of them.

'Hey!' they called behind me.

I started running. I thought one of them, at least, was running after me. I left the road and kept running into the darkness.

I'm dead. I'm dead. I'm dead. And all because of this stupid letter. Why did I do it?

Frantically, I ran, panting so hard, I felt my lungs were about to burst.

At some point, I looked back only to realise, no one was chasing me anymore. They gave up and returned to their fire. Finally, I stopped, catching my breath. But now, where was the tree where I left Tui? I thought it would be easy to find it again, but the more I looked, the more the trees looked the same. Cold panic gripped my heart. *Where is she?*

"Tui?" I called out, knowing all too well that I could now be easily found by anyone who might have still been looking for me in the dark. "Tui?" I cried, desperate.

"I'm here!" a small voice called back.

I ran towards where the voice came from. She was there, still on the lower branch.

"You're here! You're here!" I cried with relief. I helped her down and hugged her. "Tui," I said. "Tui."

"You got Rufus!" she said with delight, grabbing the bear and hugging him to her chest. "Thank you, Mummy."

"We need to run again, sweetheart," I said. "Can you run?"

"Yes."

I grabbed her hand and started running again. Away from the road, in darkness. I could hear Tui breathing heavily by my side. The ground was soggy and treacherous, growing muddier and swampier the further we got. It was becoming dangerous.

We slowed until finally we had to stop.

"Best if we tried to find the road again," I said.

I tried to navigate towards where I thought the road was, to the best of my ability, but failed.

We kept marching on. The adrenaline that pushed me to that point was slowly dissipating, and lethargy swept over me, in a sudden, unwelcome embrace. Every move was a struggle, every breath. Tui was now a couple of steps ahead. I kept my eyes on the ground, watching where I placed my feet, afraid to stumble and hurt myself in my state of complete physical and mental fatigue. The scene in the house played in my head over and over. Tears, which I managed to hold back in my state of shock and urgency, started streaming down my face.

"Are you OK, Mummy?" Tui asked, stopping in her tracks to wait for me.

"I am, sweetheart," I said faintly, as I wiped away the tears.

"Would you like to rest?" she asked, her small voice so full of concern, causing my eyes to well up again.

I looked around. We were truly in the middle of nowhere. Rows of trees stretched ahead of us, thick and lush.

"These trees would provide us with great coverage, in case we're still chased by those men," I said. "Let's just keep going."

Tui was silent. She wasn't looking at me, or at the trees ahead, but past me, her eyes fixated on something further away, her face creased with worry. I followed her gaze and gasped in fear. In the dim morning light, I could easily observe a man's figure, standing perfectly still, about one-hundred-and-fifty meters away. He was tall, his hair longer than his shoulders, and he was holding a gun.

"Let's move, hurry!" I said in some panic, grabbing her hand in mine, walking on into the trees, as fast as I could, looking back to see what the man did.

He seemed to be watching us, but he didn't chase us. Like a menacing statue, he kept watch, until the trees swallowed us, and his imposing image was gone. Still, I pushed onwards, holding Tui's hand firmly, urging her forward, fear igniting my energy reserves, until those were all spent, and I could no longer walk on.

I stopped, trying to make sure he wasn't tricking us, appearing to be gone but creeping closer. My eyes closed, I tried to still my nerves and listen for approaching steps, just as I used to do on the porch of the damned house we had only just escaped, on those nights, when I needed so desperately to be alone, breathe some fresh air, and look for the stars.

I could hear nothing. Oddly, we were alone.

"Look Mummy!" Tui said pointing to the trees. "Apples."

I couldn't hold back a smile. Yes, these were apples, and some were ripe and ready to eat. I picked two fleshy ones, and we ate them with such eagerness, ripping them and chewing, sweet apple juice dripping from our mouths. It was such a delight, an indulgence I hadn't experienced for months and months. I picked us a couple more apples and we devoured them.

My stomach gurgled. "Oh, we might have diarrhoea now," I said. "We're not used to eating apples."

Tui looked worried.

"It's OK," I said, "out here, we can just go, use leaves to wipe clean. It's what our ancestors did."

When we finally started walking again, I could see twinkling lights far ahead, beyond the trees. Carefully we made our way closer, but still far enough, so we could run if needed. The closer we got, the clearer the lights had become.

"It's a church," I said.

An old church, in the middle of nowhere. Its glassed windows were still intact, its bricks well preserved. Unharmed. These apple trees must have belonged to the worshippers.

We approached carefully, from the back. Slowly, pausing to listen for dangerous noises. But everything was calm, and peaceful. Finally, we were facing the front of the church. A large wooden door, tall and heavy, creaked open. From the inside peered the smiling, kind-looking face of a man, bald and dressed in black.

"My children; are you looking for help?" he asked.

Something about him felt honest and trustworthy, but still, I hesitated.

"It's all right. We have food here, and we have shelter. Come in," he said.

What other options did we have? Where else were we to go? I took Tui's hand and walked inside.

*

A church! That's it! A church! That's where we need to go!

First light is almost upon us, and the darkness has lifted a little. I'm still sitting on the floor in the same position, one hand on sleeping Tui, her head heavy on my thigh, the other holding the kitchen knife at the ready.

"Tui, wake up!" I say, shaking her gently. She stirs out of deep sleep, opens her eyes slowly and rolls to take a look at me.

"What's going on?" she asks, her voice croaky.

"I know where to go," I say, sounding a tad overexcited, even to myself.

"Where?"

"We need to find a church."

"Like the one we lived at after the murders?" she asks, and I shudder at how she says it, so matter-of-factly, *the murders.*

"Yes, and if we can find that same one, it would be best."

"Seriously? Even after everything that happened with that priest?"

I swallow hard. So, she knows. She's known all along.

Twenty Eight

"Please. Come inside," he said, even as we were coming inside.

I remember that moment of walking into the church, three years ago, like it was yesterday.

The church was large, for one being in the middle of nowhere. Its walls of dark grey stones towered high over the nave. The stained-glass windows, transmitting colourful light into the dim space, seemed old and delicate. It was surprising to see none were broken by the storms. Several tidy lines of pews stood at the ready to welcome worshippers, though I doubted there were that many who still came. The pulpit wasn't very high above the congregation, which made it seem more approachable. A massive, wooden communion table stood by it, with its pristine white tablecloth. Candles were lit all around, and a few wildflower bouquets in impressive large vases were placed by the east wall. Stepping inside felt as if we were transported to a place that was completely other-worldly. Death, murders, starvation, cannibalism—this place was untouched by all of that.

You could have easily thought you were a step closer to heaven, other than for the mattresses scattered on the floor, and the overwhelmed survivors that occupied some of them.

"We provide shelter to all who seek it," the priest said. "I'm Father Hubbard."

I nodded, trying my best to smile, "I'm Juniper, this is my daughter Tui."

"Hello Juniper, hello Tui. What brings you to us?"

It took me a few mumbles and stammers to finally say, "Uh, my husband and daughter were... uh, murdered." The words sounded foreign, as if I said them in Latin or Greek.

"I'm so sorry," Father Hubbard said in a tone that seemed to be genuine. "You can stay for as long as you need. We do sometimes manage to find good accommodations for people."

"How do you protect yourselves here?" I asked.

"What do you mean?" Father Hubbard asked, seeming concerned.

"From the outside world... from, all the violence?"

"Oh," Father Hubbard smiled warmly, "you mean, is it safe here?"

I nodded.

"Well, yes, it is, you have nothing to worry about. The people who live around this parish protect us. They're all armed, so we don't have to be."

I nodded, relieved. "We saw a man with a gun, just as we entered the apple orchard... we didn't realise we were going into an orchard, only when we were already there... Tui noticed the apples. We were so... distraught."

Father Hubbard nodded, still with that warm and disarming smile.

"That must have been one of our parish members. Possibly Dion Percy. He lives closes to the southern end of the orchard. A rather tall fellow, with long, grey hair?"

I nodded again. That sounded like the man I saw.

"Yes, that's him. You wouldn't've been allowed into the orchard had he deemed you threatening. He's a great shot, Dion. Ex-military. But he didn't think you came to harm us, and I don't either," he said, smiling again.

Relief washed over me.

"Here," he said and gently touched my arm to indicate free mattresses for us, but his touch made me jump. "Oh, I'm sorry, I didn't mean to scare you, Juniper," he said, looking abashed.

I felt so stupid. "It's all right," I smiled.

He walked us to our mattresses and ordered two bowls of soup to be brought for us. The soup arrived, warm and smelling divine, with chunky pieces of carrots and potatoes inside. I had to harness all my restraint not to swallow it all in a couple of insatiable gulps.

"You're hungry," Father Hubbard observed, and ordered two more bowls.

We finished them in no time as well.

As I placed the empty bowls in his hands, his thumbs touching my hand lightly, kindly, something about him, the way he looked after us, the way he cared, not looking for anything in return, made my eyes swell with tears.

"Thank you so much," I managed to whisper, as the tears

streamed down my face.

"You are most welcome," he said with a smile. He took the bowls and left us.

*

I wasn't particularly religious, but I had an inkling for spirituality, as with Tui's letter, so I joined the routine services, listening to sermons, learning from Father Hubbard how kindness to each other and to all living beings was the only thing that might save humanity. Tui joined in the beginning, but after a while she complained all services and sermons sounded the same, and stayed at our corner, reading the books Father Hubbard sourced for her.

After a week, I started helping around, sweeping floors, picking apples, digging out potatoes, planting new ones, soaking beans, preparing soup, washing clothes, even clearing the latrine. Two other families were staying in the church with us, one that was there when we came had already left. 'We found them a very nice home to go to,' Father Hubbard said.

I was in no hurry to leave. The house, the hunger, the lockdown, the murders, I couldn't face the world outside. Father Hubbard and his three deacons never even hinted at it as an option. We became part of their small parish. A woman with her two children arrived about a week after us, and a teenage young man with his younger brother. Now all the mattresses were occupied.

On Sundays, parish members would come for the service. There were about fifty of them. The man we saw by the orchard, Dion Percy, even scarier up close, was one of them. He nodded kindly to me, tipping his hat in some old, gentlemanly manner, his face grim and hard, saying absolutely nothing. They all arrived armed to the teeth, defying Father Hubbard's attempts to suggest there was no danger in God's home. They still kept their guns and knives and stood up a small guard outside.

The nights were the biggest challenge. As soon as I closed my eyes, I was thrown back into that kitchen, that dining table. I could see Moana being slaughtered again, and again, and again. Sleep was my enemy. I tried to fight it with all my might. Some nights I managed to stay up, looking at the stained-glass windows, watching as Father Hubbard was tidying up and preparing for his next service. He caught my eye once or twice, smiling. I could feel my cheeks burn like a silly schoolgirl when he did.

And there were the nights, when sleep still came, and took me back to see the horrors of my life come alive. I woke, drenched in sweat, covered in tears, my heart pounding hard.

The first night this had happened, I may have screamed. I woke up, rising from a room covered in blood, my daughter murdered on the floor, still hysterical and disoriented. Father Hubbard was there, by my side, his hand on my shoulder, comforting me. It took a few moments for me to recentre myself and realise I was safe.

"Thank you, Father," I whispered.

"Please, call me Paul," he smiled, his eyes meeting mine, radiating warmth and kindness. "Wait, I'll get you some tea," he said, and got up before I had a chance to stop him. "We make a strong brew here, that I'm sure could help you."

He returned with a steaming mug that smelled fruity and homey. I couldn't hold the tears back anymore. To be looked after like that, with my husband and daughter slain, with the world becoming so hostile and full of evil, it felt surreal. He kneeled next to me, putting his hand on my shoulder.

"It's all right, Juniper. God is still looking after you."

I wiped the tears, overwhelmed by feelings of gratitude and humility, and still strangely disoriented.

"Thank you, Father Hub… I mean, Paul. Thank you."

He smiled and lightly patted my shoulder. "Leave the mug by the mattress, it's OK. We'll clear it in the morning."

How could I not have been drawn to him? Father Hubbard, Paul, he was always there, always so kind, soft-spoken, tender; always so supportive. After the extreme evil that we had experienced, Tui and me, he was the ultimate good to balance it out. The serenity that brings hope, and kindness, and love. I missed love. I missed it so much. Even before The Great Famine and the climate catastrophe, Crispin was never this loving, never this supportive. I tried to remember, when was the last time I felt Crispin had loved me. Really loved me. It must have been before Tui was born. A long time ago. It was inevitable that my soul—and my body—strayed after Paul. I started feeling every minute he wasn't there as physical pain; I tried to organise my chores to match those he took part in. I would sit listening to the sermon, thinking he was talking only to me. My heart started beating faster when he came near. I couldn't help it. I needed his closeness. I wanted so desperately to feel the excitement of being loved, of being seen.

It was on one of the evenings, when Paul and I found ourselves at the apple orchard, by ourselves. The rain had cleared for a while, and we went to see if the trees showed signs of flowering. Sunlight had become so precarious; it wasn't taken for granted the trees would bear fruit. By then, Tui and I had been living at the church for seven months; we'd seen the apples ripen, picked, conserved, made into jams and condiments, and now awaited the fruiting cycle to restart. We were looking at the promising buds that formed on the branches. Paul was delighted, his smile was so beautiful, and I… I don't know what came over me. I kissed his lips.

Immediately I pulled myself away and started to apologise, profusely.

He laughed, not maliciously, but kindly. "It's all right, you did nothing wrong."

I didn't know where I should bury myself. What came over me?

Before I had time to assess the answer to that question, Paul took a couple of steps towards me, pulled me to him, and kissed me long and soft. I was shocked yet immensely overjoyed. I desired this. I desired him. It was such a relief to know my feelings were reciprocated. I allowed myself to melt into his lips, into his arms, my body suddenly awake, and so wanting.

As we broke off the kiss, only to stare dreamily into each other's eyes, I had to ask, "Are you going to get in trouble over this?"

He chuckled, "No. It isn't forbidden for us, we're not that sort of church."

I didn't know much about the differences between churches, but the way he said it made it sound like there was really nothing to hold us back.

The romance between Paul and me bloomed, while I did all I could to hide it from Tui. And indeed, from all the others staying at the church. Paul and I would sneak out, to the little wooden shed amidst the orchard trees, giggling like a couple of naughty teenagers, hold hands, look at the stars, kiss passionately, and make love. He was a considerate lover, and took my breath away, every time.

He was different from Crispin in so many ways. Physically, he lacked Crispin's impressive physique or his dashing charm. But unlike Crispin, Paul's attraction stemmed from his piercing eyes, and his infallible kindness. He spoke softly, slowly, deliberately, as if each word was calculated and rehearsed. It was so easy to believe he spoke the words of God. More than anything else, he exerted a kind of calm serenity, that only one who felt truly safe and secure could have done, in those days. When I was with him, the senses of safety and security that he projected washed over me, and for a moment I could stop being afraid.

I knew that, given time, I'd be falling in love with him. I could have fallen in love with him already, if only I allowed my deeply closed-off, wounded heart to unlock. Still, I entertained myself with the thought of marrying Paul. Could I be a priest's wife? Would I welcome people at the door, smile, and say 'Welcome, my children'? Would I wash his clothes and help him prepare for the sermons, make love to him every night, maybe have more children…

"We found you a lovely home," he said one morning, so surprisingly, so shockingly, I thought I could hear my world shatter on the floor, smashing into a thousand little pieces. My mouth dropped; I couldn't say a word. Sensing that Tui was watching me, expecting me to be grateful, I managed to whisper, "Oh, yes. How lovely."

That evening, Paul met me at our usual rendezvous spot, in the wooden shed.

"I feel I need to give you an explanation," he whispered, and for once, wasn't smiling his lovely, kind smile.

"You do."

"I... I must first say that this is real," he indicated with his finger at himself, and then me. "What we have, is real. I wasn't faking it," he said. "I fell in love with you. I still love you. I desire you," he said, coming close, his hand reaching for my hair. I took a step back. I needed to know why he was letting me go.

"I'm married, Juniper," he finally said.

"What?"

"She left me almost two years ago. I thought she had died. But she's come back."

I recalled the woman who walked into the church, the day before, looking dishevelled and very upset.

"Was that your wife, who came yesterday?"

"Yes, that's Maybell."

"But..." I could feel my breathing so rigid and laborious, my mind in an utter storm, "why are you taking her back? She left you!"

He smiled, somewhat sadly. "I believe this is what God expects of me," he finally said. "I am a man of God, first and foremost."

I could feel the tears streaming down my face, bitter tears of rejection and insult.

"I would have loved very much to keep you here, as my lover, my mistress," he said quietly, "but that wouldn't be fair to you, or to her. It wouldn't be God's wish."

"I don't mind..." I said. "I don't. I can stay..."

He came closer and hugged me, then kissed me again, a long and passionate kiss.

"I found the best house for you and Tui. High fences, alarm, brick walls; and I found you a job too, as an assistant at a not-for-profit organisation that helps hungry, struggling families. It won't be much, but at least you'll be able to earn some money."

I couldn't believe it was really happening. A deep sense of resentment filled me. In an instant, all the sexual tension and physical attraction Paul held over me, faded and disappeared. The sense of security that engulfed me under his wings, evaporated. All I could see was an old, pitiful man, looking for the right words as he sends his secret lover and her six-year-old daughter away.

"You're sending us away. Just like that."

"I'm not sending you away, I'm providing you with a fresh new start. A promising start."

I wanted to leave right there and then, but darkness deterred me. In the morning, Tui and I left, moved out to the beautiful brick house we made our home. For nearly three years it was our home, now taken by the storm.

Twenty Nine

Those memories of Paul and his church don't anger me anymore. On the contrary, they fill me with hope. I don't mind seeing him again. I'd known from the start of our romance that it was only a fleeting, casual thing. Otherwise, I wouldn't have tried—and clearly failed—to hide it from Tui. I wonder if he'd be happy to see me after all this time.

Daylight has broken. The sky is clear, with all signs of the tornado now gone. Tui is up, and we're about to get on our way, when I can hear movement inside the house. Damn, we should have left already, before first light. Someone is definitely here with us.

I grab Tui in my left hand, my right firmly holding the kitchen knife.

"Stay still," I whisper to her.

We can hear a few steps, then a pause; a few more steps, then another pause. The routine continues until there's someone at the door, blocking our way out.

It's a teenage boy, no more than sixteen. He's gaunt, his lean face pale, his hair cut very short, and I can see there are sores on his scalp.

He's wearing an oversized sweater, full of holes, and oversized boots that he'd probably picked from someone who'd died.

"Who are you? What're you doing here?" he asks in a voice that has only recently broken. Many young people's puberty was delayed due to malnourishment.

"We only stayed the night," I say, my knife held in front of me, at the ready. "We want no trouble."

He looks at me, completely blank, and not moving.

"Let us go through, please," I say.

"Drop your knife and I'll let you go," he says.

I wasn't going to drop the knife.

"I will not harm you," I say to him, tightening my grip on Tui's hand, "just let us get out of here, and we're gone."

"Drop the knife."

"Not a chance."

It's a Mexican standoff. None of us is moving for a couple of long drawn out minutes.

"What can you give me, then," he asks, "for letting you go?"

"Nothing. We have nothing."

"D'you have a ring? Or a necklace?"

"I don't have anything."

"I can call my friends, you'll have no chance against all of us," he says.

I don't move.

"I just need to whistle," he warns me.

I think he's bluffing, until he puts two fingers into his mouth and is getting ready to blow out a whistle. I have no chance, other than to fight our way through. I can't fight a whole gang of pubescent lads, but I might be able to move this one.

In a split-second decision I leap forward and stick the kitchen knife into his hand. I use my full force, directing all my fear and anger into the knife, then pull it out. The lad certainly wasn't expecting this. He howls in pain and shock, crouching and grabbing his injured, bleeding hand with the other one. As he bends into his pain, I push him out of the way, grab Tui and pull her behind me. Energised by extreme fear, we run through the strange house, one room leading to another, until I find the entrance.

There is a group of youngsters waiting near another house, not fifty meters away. Probably the gang he wanted to summon. We run, as fast as we possibly can.

"Yo! Don't let the bitch get away!" I can hear, behind us, the one who I stabbed telling the others.

Quite a few of them start running after us. They're howling and shrieking as they run. Pack mentality has always scared me. Never in my life had I felt more like a lamb running from a pack of wolves.

I can hear Tui breathing loudly, and I know she's already exhausted.

"Keep running," I say to her.

I'm sure they'll stop chasing us after a while, but they're still behind us.

"I'm in pain!" Tui yells to me. "My side hurts!"

"Can't stop!" I shout.

We keep running, I can hear her crying next to me, as she pushes through the pain barrier.

Suddenly, out of nowhere, there are stones falling on us, over our heads. I'm confused. There's no storm, no earthquake. Where are these stones coming from?

I sneak a look behind, and see that our chasers have stopped, and decided instead, to target us with stones. They formed a firing line, tossing large stones into the air, still howling menacingly, and yelling curses. We keep running a while longer, until we're out of their range, and out of their sight.

Finally, we stop. Tui is heaving, holding her side, crying.

"You did so well, sweetheart," I say to her, myself extremely short of breath. I always hated running.

I allow Tui a few minutes to regain her breath and strength.

"How come they stopped?" Tui wonders.

"I guess it's hard to run in shoes that are two sizes too big for you," I say. It's the only reason I can think of.

"So can we just walk now?" Tui begs.

I look back behind us. The lads have gone.

"Yes, let's just walk."

*

We've been walking for hours, and still debris from the tornado is scattered everywhere and all around us. Smashed cars, pieces of various home utensils, torn roofs, bodies. *How massive was that beast?* It wasn't the first tornado we'd had, but it was certainly the biggest, and deadliest. I still can't believe we made it out alive.

"What if another tornado starts when we're walking out here, all exposed?" Tui asks, her voice slightly shaken.

"I don't think there's another one brewing," I say. "The sky is clearer."

The road has dipped a little, and I lose sight of the horizon, suddenly worried we'd never find a shelter by nightfall. I pick up the pace but soon enough Tui is struggling to keep up behind me. I have to slow back down.

"I'm hungry," she says finally, looking lethargic. A nameless dread sneaks into my heart. I can't lose her. I can't lose Tui. I reach for her forehead, my hand shaking. No, she's cold. I exhale loudly, with some relief. Hunger I could potentially help with, but sickness is beyond my reach.

"Let's climb back up from this dip and see if we can spot a church," I say, not convinced at all there would be any to find.

We reach a high-enough point and pause. Further ahead, the road we're on continues twirling, up and down through dips and hills. I'm not sure Tui would be able to sustain such a challenging walk, down and up again, over, and over, on an empty stomach, having run to exhaustion, then walked for hours, and with such low morale. To our right, however, down below, plains stretch for several miles, meeting hills far on the horizon. Once, even before The Before, it might have been a beautiful, lush, wild forest, that was eventually claimed for a landscape of wineries, and small villages, perhaps the odd mistake of an industrial dairy farm, with its winter grazing bog. Now, it was a desert, not much more than a few congregations of small houses peppered here and there.

"There!" Tui shouts suddenly, her arm stretched, her finger pointing well into the distance.

I squint my eyes. Yes, she's right. "Definitely a church!"

*

I didn't think it'd take us so long, but the terrain is at times impassable. Treacherous mud swamps, potholes, and walls of sharp overgrown gorse to rip your skin into shreds. Tui is on the brink of fainting when we reach the first small settlement of houses. I'm half surprised to find it isn't deserted. Not exactly a hubbub of activity, but life exists here. Three elderly women are sitting together around a small tea table outside, chatting, when one of them notices us. The lively chat dies down.

"Are you lost, lovey?" one of the women, the one wearing a blue cardigan, calls to me.

"I suppose you could say that," I reply. "We survived a tornado," I add, as Tui and I get closer.

The women watch us with careful looks. I would have been suspicious of strangers just as much if I were in their place. I feel the need to explain us being there.

"We're heading to the church. We hope to find some shelter there, and some food. My daughter is so hungry."

In concert they all turn their attention to Tui. There's no way she'd be considered a threat by anyone.

After a while the women nod.

"The church is a good place," the one with the floral dress says. "Reverend Maria Toscana is such a lovely pastor," adds her friend with the wide brim hat.

Maria. Not Paul. Should I be relieved or disappointed by that? I'm not completely sure.

"Is it very much longer, to get there from here?" I ask.

"Probably an hour," says the one with the hat.

Tui hears that and drops herself on me.

"Nooooo," she exhales melodramatically.

"How old is your daughter?" asks the woman in the blue cardigan.

"She's nine."

"My granddaughter was seven," she says, and purses her lips together. I wonder what happened to her seven-year-old granddaughter. Nothing good, by the way she stopped talking and her eyes glisten.

"Wait here," her friend with the floral dress says, and walks into the house outside of which they're sitting. She returns with two glasses of water and two large carrots.

"Here," she says, and hands a glass of water and a carrot to each of us. Tui gulps the water and is already halfway through her carrot before I manage to say a heartfelt thank you.

"Oh, bless her, so famished," says the one with the hat.

"You looked after her well," says the woman in the floral dress, who fed and watered us. "You both look rather well, all things considered."

A sneaking fear of being assessed and considered as these women's next lunch chills my bones. I scan the tea table to check for sharp knives but can't see any. The fear quickly fades. They just don't seem the type. Still, I mentally connect my hand with the kitchen knife under my shirt, its blade still smudged with the young man's blood. I hand the glasses back to the woman and thank her again.

"Better be on our way," I say hurriedly. I grab Tui's hand and start walking again.

"May God preserve you," says the one in the blue cardigan, and all three of them wave.

*

This church is smaller than the other one, but it seems to have withstood the abhorrent weather pretty well. A couple of stained-glass windows are missing, patched with wooden planks instead. The front door is wide and tall, but somehow less impressive than those doors where Paul first welcomed us.

This time, it is a woman. Dressed in clergy attire, she is about my height, her short hair white, and while her smile is kind, her eyes are stern.

"Welcome," she says. "Our doors are open."

We climb the steps up to the entrance.

"I'm Reverend Maria Toscana, I'm Pastor here," she says and reaches out her hand. I grab it. Her shake is firm.

"I'm Juniper, and this is my daughter, Tui."

Tui shakes Reverend Toscana's hand feebly.

"She's very tired and hungry," I apologise.

"Are you survivors of the monster tornado or the category-five cyclone?" Reverend Toscana asks as she walks us inside.

"Category-five cyclone?"

"Well, I gather the tornado, then."

"A category-five? Here?" I wonder. I'd never heard of one so powerful to reach our shores before.

"Oh yes, that's what they say. It was a devastating hit," Reverend Toscana replies. "Just north of the hills."

North. Something in me stirs in fear. North. It's where Enav went to live, alongside the woman he fell in love with. Maybe they had children together, I didn't know. He wanted children. I'd lost touch with Enav so long ago. Why had that happened? It shouldn't have happened. We used to be so close.

"Are you OK?" Reverend Toscana asks.

"I, um, my brother, he may have been there," I mumble. "North, I mean."

"Where, exactly?"

"Well… I'm not sure."

"Do you want me to find out for you? We have a network of connections through other churches."

"Oh yes, yes please, that would be lovely."

"I'll take his details from you after you've had a chance to eat, eh?"

Reverend Toscana walks us to the kitchen. There is a long wooden table, already set for two. A deacon places two bowls of soup and a bit of bread in front of us. Tui gulps and chews loudly, as the deacon smiles.

Later, Reverend Toscana takes us to a corner where two mattresses are placed next to the wall. She hands me a sheet of paper and a pen to write Enav's name. My hand shakes as I write. I hope he's alive.

"If you wish to pray with me, just let me know," Reverend Toscana says as she takes the note from me. I nod shyly and she walks away.

Tui is already asleep on her mattress, but my mind is restless. I fear sleep. Moana and Crispin still haunt me there. I go and sit on one of the long pews. The church is silent. Cocooned within its sturdy walls, one cannot help but feel safe. I close my eyes. I want to say a prayer, but I'm not sure what to say. We need a house, we need food, we need Enav to be safe, we need the world to heal, we need so many things.

"Please watch over Tui," I whisper eventually.

*

"I have news of your brother," Reverend Toscana approaches me two days later, as I help the deacons clean the kitchen. "Come, sit down."

We sit at the long table, and I brace myself for bad news.

"First, he's alive. That's the most important thing, no?" she blurts immediately, and I sense the tightness in my chest loosen. "He works in the big quarry, not far from Maintown."

"The quarry?" I repeat.

"Yes, he's been working there for a few months now. I suppose because he had a wife and a young boy to feed."

"A boy?" I repeat, again. I can imagine a young boy, with Enav's elongated face and intelligent eyes.

"But, Juniper," Reverend Toscana continues, placing her hands on mine, in an odd, protective, maternal sort of way, "from my information, the wife and son didn't make it."

"Oh." I feel the sting of tears pricking my eyes. Enav. Dear, kind brother. What happened? Why did you leave your family to work in the quarry? My heart aches for the woman and the boy I never met. For the brother I haven't seen or spoken to in so long.

"We can pass a letter to him, if you want?" Reverend Toscana suggests.

I nod. Reverend Toscana signals with her head to the Deacon, who hurries away and returns with a pen and some papers.

"I'll leave you to it, then," the Reverend says. She's very matter-of-fact, very efficient. She lacks the radiant compassion that Paul used to ooze so effortlessly.

I sit and stare at the paper. What can I possibly write?

'Dear Enav,' I start.

No, much too formal. I scratch it out. Start over.

'Enav, my beloved brother.'

Yes, that's better.

'I try to remember why we lost touch. Was it because you hated,'

No, cross out hated.

'...disliked Crispin so much? I'm not sure anymore. You used to be the most important person in my life. I miss you. Tui is now nine years old. She'd love to meet her uncle. I don't think you've seen her more than twice. You never met Moana. She was taken from me, together with Crispin, three years ago. Murdered in front of my eyes. But Tui and I are fine. We'll find a new place to live soon, and I'll ask Maria (the priest of this church where we're currently staying), to make sure you have the new address.

Please come and visit us, Enav. I want you to be part of Tui's life. Why not come over for Christmas? It's five months away and I'm sure we'll have a place of our own by then. We can talk then, about everything we missed in each other's lives.

I've been told you had a little boy. I'm so sorry, Enav. I want to hug you. I'll be looking forward to seeing you again, hopefully during Christmas like I proposed.

Love and hugs from your little sister, Juniper.'

I quickly add,

'...and your beautiful niece, Tui.'

When Reverend Toscana returns to collect the written letter, the pen, and the unused papers, I pluck up my courage and say, "Reverend, sorry, I must ask…"

She turns her full attention to me. "Yes?"

"Three years ago, Tui and I stayed in a church, much like this one, a little bigger actually. They were very kind to us, we were… sort of, refugees, yeah, like we are now, I suppose."

I stumble on my words, not sure how to phrase my question. Already I sound like a complete idiot.

"There was a very nice man, a priest, I mean. He was very kind. His name was Father Hubbard…"

"Father Paul Hubbard?" Reverend Toscana interrupts. "Yes, he was a lovely man."

Was. She said was. Did I hear her right?

"Was?" I ask hesitantly, hoping to be wrong.

"Oh, yes. Sadly, he passed, about a year ago. One of those viruses that no one seems to know where they came from or how to get rid of," Reverend Toscana says, her sorrow somehow not deep enough to be completely believable. "We lost a wonderful priest."

"Uh, yes. He was wonderful, he was," I say, as I bite the lips he used to kiss so softly, my throat thick with painful sorrow.

*

It isn't long before the Reverend comes over to propose a house that has sadly been vacated by its residents due to famine and disease.

"It's a lovely area, no more than half an hour's walk from the monthly market," she says.

"A monthly market?"

"Oh yes, The Great Famine is dead in the water, I believe, praise the Lord."

I want to share in her joy, but I can't. The famine may have been won by sheer determination and the immense investments of a few, but the wrath of the climate is not about to halt. Ferocious tornados, now extreme cyclones, relentless rain, mudslides, landslips, and floodings, these were still coming thick and fast at us.

I remember a day as a child spent on the beach with Enav. We were playing around, hopping on rocks, observing some crabs, counting all the dead fish we could find. There were many. Too many.

Enav told me then that sea life was expected to become extinct by twenty forty-eight. It was this year. Twenty forty-eight was now. And the fish were nearly all gone, just like he said.

When we were kids, there was a big campaign that called on people to stop using plastic drinking straws, to save the fish. But people never stopped eating fish to save the fish. When confronted with sights of dead dolphins and sea turtles who swallowed and choked on plastic, people got enraged. But they never bothered directing that rage towards overfishing, with plastic nets and long hooks being the main cause of sea life choking. For years, world leaders had failed to fight and save whales, some already endangered, from being slaughtered mercilessly in a sea that was long before declared an international sanctuary. Only one, small, heroic organisation, under the brave Captain Paul Watson, fought to save them. And now, indifference had come back to bite us. Everything was about to come crashing down over our heads, even if food was less scarce now.

Nothing was dead in the water, except for those who were dead in the water.

*

It's the morning Tui and I leave the church for our new home, and Reverend Toscana is standing on the front stone-porch to bid us farewell.

"May God preserve you," she says, then adds, "And always remember, you have a place here, with us."

"Thank you, thank you so much for your kindness," I say.

As we make to leave, a big van arrives. The driver, a large man with a short, grey beard, jumps out of the van, and says only one word, "Bodies."

I look back at Reverend Toscana, slightly horrified.

"We provide them with a mass burial," the Reverend explains. "We don't know their names. If we do, we bury them separately, with a named cross."

I nod. The man is already pulling out bodies from the back of the van and onto a cart.

"A grave has been dug already, Freddy, at the back. Just take them straight in," the Reverend tells him. "I'll come soon to offer prayers over them."

Solemnly, Tui and I walk past. The stench of rotting flesh is wretched, and we have to cover our noses and mouths in revulsion.

Still, in direct contrast to my will to get away from there as soon as possible, I stop in my tracks as I see a small red-headed person being taken out. Tui keeps on walking ahead, putting as much distance as possible between herself and the bodies before she turns around and waits for me. But I can't move. There's another, larger, red-headed person already on the cart; that's the woman we met after the storm. And the little one being now taken out, that must be her boy she lost.

"What happened to her?" I ask the man from behind my covered nose and mouth.

"Not sure," he says, his face completely uncovered, as if he has no sense of smell at all. He neatly places the child on his mother.

"Found her dead on the road. I think she may have killed herself, see?"

He stops to grab her hand, to show me the wrists, deeply cut, with dried blood all over. "I reckon she did it herself."

He then takes a close look at me. "Why? D'you know her?"

"I don't know her name. We met her after the storm," I say, sadly. "Where did you find the boy?"

"Miles away. Was skewered to a tree, took ages to retrieve. Poor little bugger," he says calmly. "Know his name?" he asks.

I look at the smaller body, and my stomach turns. Already he's decomposed enough to make his childish face bloated and alien like. What must have been delicate, sweet features, have eroded, except for his lovely red hair. It's the same colour as the woman's. It must be Sammy. It must be. But if I tell him the name, they'd take him away. Sammy will be buried separately, that's what Reverend Toscana had said. Deep in my heart, I strongly feel that separating them would be the wrong thing to do. The boy should be placed with his mother. For a split second I ponder whether to make up a name for her, but I immediately rule it out. Somehow, giving her a false identity seems wrong.

"No, I'm sorry," I whisper, "I don't know."

"Oh, well, it's the mass grave for them, then," the man says as he keeps pulling bodies from the van, and onto the cart.

"At least they have a grave," I say.

It's more than what Crispin and Moana had.

FIVE

YEARS

EARLIER:

2043

Thirty

Moana is finally asleep. I'm at my wits' end with that girl. I don't know what to do.

I never imagined being so bad at it, motherhood. Since I was a young girl, I knew I wanted to have children. I was looking forward to it, having children of my own. I thought I did a marvellous job with my stuffed bear toy.

I knew I'd have a girl. I'd always known.

Only—it was always Tui that I'd been waiting for. I knew she'd come, just as I'd known the sun was going to rise the next morning, and Mum was about to wake me up to go to school. I was waiting for her, my Tui. Anticipating her.

Moana, she's the surprise test I desperately fail at, and keep failing, with every day passing.

I'm so tired.

I have such a strong urge to open the door, step outside, and take a deep breath of fresh air. If it isn't raining again, I'd like to look to the sky and see if I can observe some stars tonight. Thick clouds often mask them, but maybe tonight I'd be able to see the moon. I'm too scared to open the door. This neighbourhood is dangerous. Revealing myself to the world on the front porch might well end with me stabbed, or shot, accidentally or deliberately.

Still, there are nights when I don't care, I just have to take one small step outside the door. I'm overcome with the need to put some distance between me and the inside of that homely prison.

With shaking hands, I unlock the front door. I make sure the house is dark before I carefully, slowly, twist the handle and push the door open, only a smidgen. I smell the outside to establish whether any cars have been lit close by. I tune in my ears to listen to rude conversations and wild laughter in the vicinity. Only then, when all is clearly still and there is no one around to notice, I open the door, just enough to squeeze myself through it. I duck, and sit on the porch, as low as possible but with my chest still widely stretched to allow a deep intake into my lungs, and I breathe. Deep and long, over, and over, waiting until I'm recentred and I can go back inside.

Sitting on the porch, listening to potential approaching threats, I hear some glass shatter in the distance, and someone yelling. It's still far enough away, and I decide to stay outside for a little while longer. I remember the days, long gone, when you didn't need to fear your neighbours. I smile to myself at memories of a potluck barbecue Mum organised for our street neighbours when I was a kid. We didn't know those neighbours at the time, yet some came, and we didn't fear them. They weren't threatening, only boring, driving Enav and me to leave the party and go to the beach.

Enav. I wonder where he is and how he's doing. I miss him so much.

I don't think either of us made a deliberate decision not to be in touch with the other anymore. It's not something either of us would have done. We loved each other. We were each other's rock in the challenging days of Mum's battle with cancer. As Mum was slowly declining, so was our bond. I'm not even sure how, but I found myself leaning more and more on Crispin instead. Maybe that was the problem.

Gosh, he was so dashing then, Crisp. The college rugby star that all the doe-eyed girls wanted. Suddenly it was me and him, and I was infatuated, and flattered. I needed that outside porch to sneak out to when things with Mum became too much to take. Crispin was my porch. I don't think Enav understood that. He never liked Crispin.

I close my eyes and try to focus on my breathing. I stay perfectly still, savouring every moment I have, on my own, unseen. Suddenly, I'm alert. I can hear footsteps down the road, and by the sound of it, it's more than one person. I quickly sneak back inside the house, and remain by the door, breathing hard with fear. I can hear the men talk to each other; one blurts some banter, and the others laugh enthusiastically, but I can't make out what they're saying. They pause for a while in front of the house. I try to assess how long it would take me to leap to the bench and grab a kitchen knife. Could I do it before they barge in? I tense and get ready to pounce, my teeth clenched so hard I can feel pain radiating into my jaw. To my relief, they decide to keep on walking.

I exhale with relief, just as Moana starts crying in her bed. She hardly ever sleeps through the night. Often, she wets the bed too. Every night, I pile towels under her small body to soak it. Washing sheets—washing anything—is such a mammoth chore, with hardly any soap and no washing machine. I soak everything in the tub, then hang it on makeshift washing lines that Crispin hung above the tub. There's no point hanging anything outside; nothing would ever dry in the constant rain, and whatever might, will be stolen.

I'm so tired.

"What is it, darling?" I say and check underneath her body. She's dry, thank goodness. I don't think I could face washing towels and bedding right now.

"She's hungry, Mummy," Tui peeps from the bed.

"I know, sweetheart," I say, as I pull my hair into a ponytail, frustrated, "I know."

I'm so tired.

All I can offer the girls right now is warm water mixed with some sugar. I check our dwindling sugar supply and shudder. I must ask Crispin to find more.

It takes Moana another hour to calm down, until she's finally asleep again.

I'm so tired. I can't remember falling asleep.

I wake up, abruptly, to Crispin's hand shaking me. What does he want? I'm still so sleepy. What time is it?

"You forgot to lock the door, Juniper," he says, looking angry. "Where is your mind?"

"I, I don't know. I'm sorry."

"No, it's not good enough, Jun. You can't leave the door open like that. One day…who knows what might happen!"

"I'm sorry. I…Moana started crying…I just wasn't thinking."

"No, you weren't!"

"It won't happen again, I promise."

FIVE

YEARS

EARLIER:

2038

Thirty One

I look into his big, brown, clever eyes. They are sad, dim, and tired. He can barely raise himself. The disease has finally won.

All the long nights I whispered in his sweet ears, "Fight it! Please, Johnny, fight it!" and he listened, he fought. I was so hopeful that he'd make it one more Christmas, one more year. The medications he took were expensive, but I kept buying them for him. The little I got as inheritance after Mum died helped, one cancer victim's money paying for another. Crispin was very generous too, covering some of it himself, paying from his meagre teacher's salary. Enav, still such a lost soul, tried to help, whenever he was paid for his random jobs, but it was always so little. Yet all of us together, we managed.

I was so careful to give Johnny every pill and every potion at the exact prescribed time. Some were to be given on an empty stomach and some on full, some I powdered and hid in his food, and some poured into his mouth. I sat and patted his beautiful coat, talking to him softly, words of love and encouragement. He was shedding fur at an alarming rate; his body mass shrank, and he felt brittle.

The fight was drawn out of his weak body.

"Are you ready?" the vet nurse says, placing her hand gently over my hand.

How can I be ready? I'm not ready. I'll never be ready. I can't bear the thought of not having him by my side anymore.

"I just want him back," I whisper.

"Sorry?" She's not sure if what she'd heard was what I said.

"I wish I could have him back," I say, a little louder, "as before. As he was."

"I understand," she replies kindly. I bet she does. I'm sure she has seen hundreds of people like me, hundreds of dogs like Johnny, just like this, as we are, on the brink of goodbye.

"Do you still want to wait for your brother to come?" she asks, looking at her watch, clearly wanting to get it over and done with.

We've been waiting for almost an hour. I don't think Enav is coming. I'm alone.

I'm alone.

You used to be at my side, always at my side, Johnny.

But now I'm alone.

I nod feebly to the nurse.

Within a few seconds, he breathes his last, held in my arms, and I burst into uncontrollable wailing.

"No, no, no," I cry.

The vet nurse, who must have seen hundreds of scenes just like this one, comes and hugs me kindly.

"I'll give you a few moments with him," she says and disappears behind the door.

Suddenly the clinic seems cold and sterile. Everything feels alienating; even the blanket his body is lying on isn't very soft or comfortable. I didn't notice all that before. I lean towards him, stretch my arms over his lifeless body, tears still running down my face. I'm surprised at how quickly his body starts to cool.

"I'm sorry I couldn't help you more," I whisper into his ears. He used to prick them up when I whispered to him, but now they remained flat, unresponsive.

"What would you like to do with him, now?" the vet nurse asks as she returns into the room.

"Pardon?"

"Would you like to take him and bury him, or do you prefer to cremate him?"

"I, I don't know. I need to ask my brother."

"OK, that's not a problem. We can keep him here for you until you decide."

*

"Definitely cremate," Crispin says when he comes home, finding me on the bed, destroyed by grief.

"I need to ask Enav," I say.

"Enav?" Crispin blurts. "He'll probably say you need to put him on a zeppelin and fly him to Mars, or something weird like that."

"No, he won't," I say, hugging my pillow. I can feel Tui's letter underneath it. *You'll never know Johnny, Tui. You'll never have the complete pleasure and joy of meeting him.*

"When will you ask him?" Crispin wondered. "I bet it costs money, keeping Johnny in storage."

In storage. Like some chattel. A thing.

"Tomorrow."

But a knock on the door disrupts me from sinking into deeper, all-encompassing sorrow. It's Enav.

"Where have you been?" I shout at him, my sadness easily projected as fury.

"I'm sorry," he says, "I was stuck at work, they wouldn't let me leave. I couldn't call you; the network is so dodgy. I couldn't get a line."

"You left me there by myself!" I shout, not hearing him. Not caring what he had to say.

"I thought Crispin might have been there," he looks at Crispin, slightly accusingly.

"Hey, don't put this at my doorstep, mate," Crispin replies, agitated. "I couldn't leave school."

"Well, I couldn't leave the BioFuel station," Enav responds, equally agitated.

"You work at the BioFuel station now?" Crispin asks, his tone slightly arrogant.

I bet they'll be slipping into a 'whose job is more important' competition now. I can't bear it.

"It doesn't matter," I say, loudly, to cut them both off. "It's done. He's gone."

They both look at me, silently. We all share this sadness. We all loved Johnny.

"Now we need to decide what to do with his body," I continue, quietly.

"I thought we agreed to cremate him," Enav says, and Crispin is so visibly relieved. No zeppelin to Mars then.

*

Finally, the rain has stopped for a few days, allowing Enav and me to scatter Johnny's ashes. I didn't want to scatter them, I wanted to keep him in the lovely wooden box we were given by the vet clinic, but Enav was adamant that we should scatter. He insisted that it was as much his decision as it was mine, since Johnny belonged to both of us, as children, even if we weren't living under the same roof anymore, and Johnny had spent the last two years living with Crispin and me.

"He isn't just your dog," Enav said, "and I think scattering his ashes would be a better decision."

"Why?"

"Because he was a free spirit, and with all these floods, moving from house to house, what if you leave him behind one day? Isn't it better that we return him to the earth? Free?"

The floods were intensifying, and Enav had a point. Life was very clearly growing harder due to the climate changing so violently, and who knew what was going to happen to us all? Tui's letter I could carry in my pocket, but Johnny's ashes, in the beautiful wooden box, were harder to shove in there.

"You don't actually mean to scatter him, do you?" Crispin was horrified at the idea.

"I think we do."

"Your brother is being foolish, and way too demanding, Jun. Why can't you stand up to him? Tell him we're not scattering and that's that!"

"Crispin doesn't want us to scatter," I told Enav.

"Johnny wasn't Crispin's dog, Juniper! It isn't his decision to make," Enav was becoming impatient.

"Crispin looked after him these past two years, Enav. He was here for Johnny when he got sick, you weren't!"

"He wasn't his dog! Why can't you stand up to him?"

"That's what he asked me, about you."

I was sick and tired of being the pawn, tossed around between these two men. So, in the end, I decided to side with Enav. Johnny's spirit was already released back to the universe; there was no point holding onto his ashes when the future was so uncertain.

Crispin wasn't pleased with that at all, but in the end, Johnny wasn't his dog, as Enav said. He was mine, mine and Enav's. It was our decision.

"Crispin isn't coming?" Enav asks, as we walk up the hill.

With no rain, and a glimpse of some sunrays peeping occasionally through the thick clouds, everything feels fresh, clean, and beautiful. For a brief moment, I'm filled with hope. A shot of endorphins fires in my brain. How can the future be as bleak as they say, with days such as this? With green hills, wildflowers, and my brother by my side, just like it was when we were kids.

"No, he's teaching."

We keep walking silently, looking for the perfect spot to open the box and let Johnny be one with the wind.

"Are you happy, Juniper?" Enav asks me suddenly.

"What? Why?"

"I'm serious, are you happy? With him?"

He means Crispin, obviously.

"You really don't like him, eh?"

"It's not that, Sis. You know it. I have nothing against the bloke. I just," he pauses in search for the right words. "I never thought he was right for you, you know that."

"I know, but I still don't understand why."

"I think you can do better, that's all. I want you to be happy."

"He loves me, Enav. And I love him."

"And are you happy?"

I don't know how to answer that. Am I happy? What does it

mean? Is anyone happy, always? Do we know when we are? Or is it just something you feel when you look back on bygone days, when you remember olden times, and finally you realise, you were happy then.

"I'm not unhappy," I say.

Enav looks at me, and after a while he nods. He's not meaning to upset me.

We reach the top of the hill in silence.

"I think this is a good spot," Enav says. "What do you think?"

I look around. The valley below has been hit hard by the constant rainfall, and the repeated floods. But still, it looks so beautiful, and I refuse to sink into despair.

"Yes, it's good."

Enav wrestles with the wooden box for a while. It's so tightly shut. Finally, he manages to unhinge the seal and the top comes off. Johnny's ashes come swirling in the wind and spread in the air, some fly away beyond our reach, and some spin all around us; some on us. I quickly wipe Johnny's final remains off my coat, and see him disappear between the flowers, and onto the ground.

"Goodbye, my love," I call behind him. In my mind I can hear him barking back.

*

We walk back down the hill, both of us quiet and withdrawn.

"I'm pregnant." I finally say what I'd wanted to tell him since the morning.

"What?"

"I'm pregnant, Enav. I'm going to have a baby."

"Oh, uhm, congratulations."

"It's Tui."

"It's what?"

"Tui. Remember?"

He looks as if he's trying to remember something important but fails.

"Don't you remember? Tui!"

"Oh, wait, is that the baby girl you said you'll have? When we were kids?"

"Yes!"

"Oh," he says as if it's of no importance.

"It's her, Enav! The girl I've been waiting for. I knew she'd come. She's here," I say and pat my navel gently. "She's finally here."

"I thought it was just a name you really liked," he says, a little confused.

"No. It was a whole person," I'm getting a little annoyed. How could he not remember how important she was to me?

"Remember the letter?" I ask.

"Letter?"

"Oh, come on! The letter you dictated for her, that day on the beach!"

"I'm sorry, Sis, I…" he shakes his head.

He doesn't remember.

"I wrote her a letter. I still have it," I say, my enthusiasm and excitement fading.

"That's lovely," he replies, clearly unaware of the weight of this letter, of my anticipation for this child. This exact child, not a namesake. Her.

He coughs, uneasy. "When are you due?"

"Early next year," I say.

"Twenty thirty-nine," he says. "Sounds like a good year to be born in."

I don't know what he means by that.

"Does Crispin know?" he finally asks.

"Not yet."

"Aren't you going to tell him?"

"Yes, today."

"I'm flattered," he smiles.

"About what?"

"That you told me first."

I didn't plan it that way. I thought because it was Tui, not just any baby, Enav would be excited, because he'd remember. But he doesn't, and now it means nothing that I told him first.

I shrug.

"I also have news," he says. I look at him, surprised.

"I'll be moving around the country, with my job at the BioFuel station. They need drivers, and I need a good job. It pays well."

"Because of the danger!" I burst out. BioFuel was getting so outrageously expensive; people couldn't afford it anymore. BioFuel truck drivers were routinely ambushed, taken at gunpoint, the trucks they drove stolen, their bodies occasionally found, often not.

"I'll have a gun with me, and a knife," he says. "You should see the knife, pfff…" he says, and sounds like a little boy. "It can slice you top to bottom in one strike."

I can't match the person talking to me with the words I hear him say. I can't picture Enav with a gun, or a knife. It saddens me that he'd found himself needing to use these.

"You wanted to be an opera singer," I say.

"As a child. As a joke."

"It wasn't a joke, you were serious."

"And what would I be doing these days as an opera singer, Sis, eh? What's left of music and arts these days?" He's clearly upset. "Nothing. That's what. Everywhere there's war. Everywhere there's hunger and poverty. One place has no water, so people kill each other; another place has too much water, so people kill each other. They say we're on the verge of a great famine here too. Soon people will have nothing to eat, and trust me, they'll be killing each other for that too. What would an opera singer do?"

I don't know. I didn't see it that way. I was so contained in my own life, my world seemed to be continuously defined and framed by the sorrow of others. First Mum, then Johnny. I didn't see the bigger picture.

"I know so little about the world," I finally say.

Enav smiles. "Just look after that baby of yours. Focus on that."

I smile back.

"Look after yourself too, Enav. Be careful."

"I will."

Thirty Two

I'm heavy, my tummy is bulging, and there's a funny, dark line, that runs from my chest all the way down to my crotch. I feel the sweat gathering under my hairline, between my full and sore breasts, and in the nook over my tailbone. The simplest activity exhausts me and wiping mud from walls and furniture isn't the simplest activity.

*

The house had been flooded again. The rain had battered us for days on end, unrelenting, unforgiving. I'd lain awake in bed, uncomfortable in my largeness, feeling Tui kicking, listening to the onslaught of the storm on our roof, expecting it to cave in on us sooner rather than later. Flood waters came gushing into the community, taking everything in their path with them—cars, trees, boats, animals, some whole houses, and humans.

Crispin rushed to the District Disaster Response Centre and brought home a truckload of sandbags to place around the house. His resourcefulness helped but didn't completely prevent the water from coming inside. A formidable river of mud that wasn't there before, was running so high I feared it might spill through the windows. We had nowhere to go. Enav was moving from place to place with the BioFuel truck, and Mum's house had been taken by the sea long ago. We had to stay, until a team of Response Centre rescuers came to pull me out through the window, onto a floating rescue boat, and from there to a large hall where others like me had spent several nights, worried, consumed with fear and uncertainty.

I wasn't able to sleep. Not worried for the house, but for Tui. I wondered how all this stress affected her development. Being so pregnant, I couldn't crouch all the way down to the mattress that I was offered on the floor, so I perched on the most comfortable chair I could find instead.

"Have some tea, love." A nice, middle-aged woman came over, offering me a dark brew in a glass mug.

I smiled and took it from her with gratitude.

"When are you due?"

"Four weeks," I said, hoping Tui didn't decide to push her way out early.

"Do you know what you're having?"

"A human," I replied and laughed, but the woman didn't seem to share my humour. "A girl," I said.

We've never checked. I had no scans, no tests. The health system was crumbling as it was, with the first clear signs of a critical hunger problem that officials were careful not to name famine. The deepening lack of resources due to continental and civil wars in so many places, meant imports and exports were pretty much at a standstill. I wasn't worried about not being seen by a professional, though, I didn't feel like I needed it. I knew it was a girl. I knew who it was. I knew she'd be safe. I've been waiting for her my whole life.

I was becoming more and more aware of how strange it sounded to others. Even Crispin just didn't get it. He begged me to go and see a midwife. There was one living down the street, only a few houses from us. Eventually, after all his pleadings, I went to see her. She was a nice woman of about fifty, plump and pleasant, who looked happy to see me and even happier to come over and help me with my labour.

"You are doing very well," she said after a short examination, mainly of my blood pressure and the thickness of my ankles, "and your baby seems to be doing very well too. Its heartbeat is steady and strong. Well done, Mama!"

'Its'…

Don't say 'its', say 'her'.

Tui.

No, the midwife wouldn't understand it either.

*

Finally, a break in the rainfall has allowed us to return home and start swiping the water out. Through some connections at the Disaster Response Centre, Crispin managed to source a pump that he used for clearing the house of the swamp that has taken hold inside. It took a few days to clear all the water and dry the floor.

Now all that is left is to clean the mud from the walls, the shelves, and the legs of the furniture. It's what I'm doing.

"Are you all right, Jun?" Crispin looks at me, worried. "Why don't you take a break, sit down. I can do it."

I'm happy for a break, but work distracts me from thinking about the impending labour and my mind drifts away from the pain that starts zapping me, from my lower back all the way around my navel, to my chest.

I keep wiping the walls until the pain intensifies so much, I can't ignore it.

"Crispin!"

He's at my side in a flash, helping me straighten, rubbing my back.

"Are you alright? Has it started?" he asks in a mixture of both worry and excitement.

I nod and moan with pain. Suddenly, a flush of warm water drips to the floor between my legs.

"My water just broke," I say, as my hands grab the back of the dining chair, bending forward to ease the pain.

"Shall I get the midwife now?" Crispin asks.

"Yes!" I say, as another wave of pain fires through me. "Get her now."

Within moments Crispin is back with the midwife. Both fuss around me with a relentless stream of questions, suggestions, and advice. I'm led around the house to walk off the pain, then I'm made to bend over the chair, then lie down on the bed, which is the worst.

"Please, please," I finally say, as loudly as I can without shouting, "let me."

They hush and look at me, puzzled. I raise myself off the bed and walk around for a while, unsupported, humming to myself. I let the sound of my own voice drown my pain. Come on Tui, come on, it is your time. I can feel her. I know she understands me. I crouch in the middle of the dining room, my hands holding the chair. The midwife comes to my assistance, but truth is, I don't need much help. It's almost as if I've done it before, many times over.

Though I fear Crispin might faint at any moment.

*

"Here you are! Tui. My Tui. Welcome to the world, my precious little girl. I've been waiting for you. Gosh, I've been waiting for you for so long, and here you are. So precious. So beautiful. I'll do anything to protect you, to shield you from harm and evil.

Look! I wrote you a letter! A long, long, time ago... I was only a child myself, but I already knew you'd come. One day I'll give it to you, my child. For now, just take my breast and drink. Yes, that's the way, good girl. Here, put your head on me, yeah, just like that, you're so smart, already you know what to do. I love you, sweetheart. My Tui."

Thirty Three

Holding you in my arms, Tui, watching you sleep so contentedly on my chest, listening to your precious little breaths, feeling the warmth of your body against mine, I can't help wishing Mum was here to see you. She would have loved you, I'm sure of it.

It's been three years since Mum succumbed to the sickness, and I miss her.

It was always just the three of us, Mum, Enav, and me. Dad left when I was a small baby. I never knew much about him, other than he worked on a supply ship that went back and forth to and from either Asia or the Middle East. We only had a couple of faded photos of him—one in which he held baby Enav, the other on his own in the front garden. I hated him for leaving us.

Mum was our rock, our guardian, and our disciplinarian. The small house on the beach was our haven, and our kingdom, or shall I say, queendom. With its salt-eaten cladding and once-red roof, the large windows were always wide open, to allow the breeze in, the chequered red and white curtains neatly tied to the sides, so they didn't blow unruly. Inside, the wooden walls were covered almost floor to ceiling with stuff on display: photos, pictures, and shelves covered in trinkets of all kinds. Mum was a bit of a hoarder. The worn carpet was dated and the wallpaper a yellowy shade, but it all fitted together.

The back of the house faced the sea. Enav and I would run down the set of stairs that ended on solid ground, but that within less than fifty meters turned to soft, light, grainy sea sand. Sand was an integral part of our lives, as it was everywhere. Each morning we saw Mum painstakingly wipe the benches, lifting all her many trinkets and bits and bobs, to wipe underneath, wipe the table, and picture frames, of the sand that had settled on them the previous day. Still, she'd never shut the windows. That proximity to the wildness of the sea made her happy.

"Nothing healthier than the sea breeze, Jun. Breathe deeply and slowly, it will make you strong," she'd say.

We spent so much time on the beach, Enav and I. At a very young age, Mum taught us to swim, and was pretty laid back about us going deep into the water. The sea was our friend; we weren't afraid of it back then. Straight after school, dropped off back home by the cranky, fuming school bus, we'd throw our backpacks on the porch, take our shoes off by the front door entrance, and run to the beach. It was our playground. We'd go looking for crabs between the rocks and see if the shallow water had locked some fish that needed to be rescued. We'd play dragon and dragon-slayer, or Robinson Crusoe finds Friday, or Treasure Island. Enav would sing against the wind, with a deep, pompous, operatic voice, and I'd laugh at his silliness. Then, after we adopted Johnny, he'd run with us onto the beach, barking loudly, happily, and dive into the cool water after us. As evening came, Mum would stick her head out the back window and call us for dinner, and we'd pretend we couldn't hear her. We'd take another half an hour before we finally rushed back, the sun having been swallowed by the sea.

It was the happiest childhood. I wish I could give you such a childhood, Tui.

But I'm afraid the sea has turned against us. We didn't notice it at first. Everyone was talking about climate change and the rising sea waters, but it was some grown-up's fairy tales, something you'd hear on the news but only affecting some island countries that I never heard of before, somewhere in the South Pacific. I never thought it could affect us.

But it did. Slowly, the sea started creeping closer to the house. Sneakily, stealthily, we didn't even notice it to start with. Until rain started falling, and it kept falling, and falling, and falling. It wouldn't stop. Suddenly, there was no clear boundary between rainwater pooling on the road at the front of the house, and the sea water in the back. And even when the rain had finally stopped, the sea wouldn't recede. Steadily, golden sand was eaten by hungry waves, wild and foamy, breaking steadily closer to the house, steadily higher, steadily more powerful. Our friend had become hostile, and dangerous.

Maybe that's why Mum got sick.

I was twenty years old, first year student of law at the university. Mum always said I should be a lawyer, and Enav always agreed.

"The way you talked me into keeping Johnny was clear proof you should practice law, Jun," Mum kept saying. "You could have talked a robber out of a prison sentence."

I loved university life. I loved the large faculty buildings, the way they smelled from the inside, a little damp, a little old, with their creaking floors and red-carpeted staircases. I loved the high-ceilinged library, the hush that was always forced, the wide study tables. I loved the lecture halls, and the lectures, the cafeteria, and the park. I loved to be with my friends, a group of smart, ambitious, driven people I had only met at the start of the year and already liked so much. I loved the dormitories, my small room with the single bed and the square window. I loved the way it felt mine, even though scores of students had lived there before me. I loved the way I'd decorated it, with photos of Mum and Enav and Johnny, and some posters that I liked. I loved going to the pub. I loved the study groups. I loved everything about it.

It was on one of the lively pub visits, with my law student friends, that I met Crispin. We'd been to high school together but were practically strangers to each other back then. Seeing him again suddenly, handsome, tall, I was instantly drawn to him. He was in his final year of studies, soon to become a teacher.

"Hey, you," he approached me, holding a pint of beer, smiling widely, looking confident and beautiful, "didn't we go to high school together?"

I could feel my neck and my cheeks burning. "Yeah," I said, giggling foolishly.

"I'm Crispin," he said, leaning a little bit into me.

"Juniper," I replied, a little too keenly.

"That's such a beautiful name, Juniper. Juniper." He rolled the name on his tongue a few times, slightly intoxicated. "Very beautiful name for a very beautiful girl."

I giggled.

"What's your major?" he asked.

"Law."

"Oh, beautiful *and* smart. That's awesome."

I still giggled.

"I'm going to be a teacher."

"Oh, that's cool. What will you be teaching?"

"Dunno yet. Maybe math."

"I'm sure the students are going to love you," I said, sounding immediately stupid to myself.

"Yeah, I'm good with kids," he replied.

I smiled, sipping my beer, loving the attention but somehow lost for words.

"So, uh, a bunch of us are going to watch the rugby tomorrow, d'you want to come? With me, I mean? D'you want to come with me?"

I nodded, perhaps too enthusiastically, turning my head only slightly to see my law student friends cheering me on ecstatically over their beers, making some grotesque sexualised hand gestures to match.

And that was it. Your Dad and I became a couple. Crispin was that good-looking type of guy who could really get away with things only because of how he looked, and his forced charm. He'd gate-crash into my dormitory after curfew, get caught on the way out, and walk away scot-free, not a scratch on his unscathed reputation. It took a long time, and the entire world to have changed, for his rugby-star aura to fade. I was so infatuated with him.

Every other weekend I'd take the bus home, to visit Mum and Johnny. Enav was traveling in the deep south, still looking for his life's calling. For years he'd dreamt of spending time in some exotic, faraway land, but the cost of fuel meant that only multimillionaires could afford to fly. He'd had to settle for a local ashram and some solo nature trekking.

Every time, as the bus took the curve around the bend in the single lane road that led to our home, and the house was at once made visible, I'd feel a tinge of surprise at how everything had changed in such a short time. The sea came steadily closer, making the house look so small and fragile. More of the sand was gone. Even the bus had to drive very slowly here, since seawater started to continuously splash over the asphalt. I feared it was only a matter of time before the road became impassable.

And then, to top all my worries, came that one time I returned home for a visit, to find the back window, the one facing the sea, closed. My heart instantly sank.

I stepped off the bus, my knees buckling, knowing deep inside that something was wrong.

Johnny, as he always did, rushed out through the open front screen door that was never locked, barking and wiggling, jumping up and down, covering me with his happy slobber.

"Hello, my darling boy, hello, hello, hello," I said with that voice that was saved only for him, as I rubbed and petted his lush fur.

Mum did not follow him out, as she frequently did, so, I stepped into the house, immediately knowing that something was off. Our home was always one to vibrate with that special feeling, Mum used to call 'joie de vivre'. I never quite understood what she meant, until I grew up. It was that essence of a feeling that you'd just walked into a happy home, where people who love life reside. It's not that we were never sad, or cross, or disappointed, but the deeply vibrating love of life was always stronger than that. Even Dad's deserting us did not affect that; 'It's what created it,' Mum said.

But now, I stepped in a house where that feeling of joie de vivre was missing. Some of the windows were closed, some curtains were drawn together. There was no smell of vegetables cooking on the stove, no music playing.

"Mum?" I called into the house, thinking maybe she wasn't home. Life was still safe enough that the front door was often left unlocked.

"Here Jun!" Mum called back from her bedroom.

I walked inside quickly, not kicking off my shoes as I always had, Johnny still obliviously happy by my side. Mum was lying in her bed; the room was dim with the curtains drawn together. Mum's face was very pale, almost grey, with dark circles under her beautiful eyes.

"Mum? What's going on?"

"Hi Jun. Come in, come in, fetch the chair."

I dragged the chair that stood by her vanity, and positioned it as close to her as I could.

"What's going on, Mum?"

She reached with her hand to mine. Her hand felt heavy, and cold.

"Oh, Jun. I didn't want to worry you," she said, even her voice sounding pale and grey.

"Well, too late, I'm worried now. What's the matter?"

"I'm uh, sick."

"Sick? Like what, the flu?"

"No, no," she smiled, a tired smile. "I have cancer, Jun."

Her eyes met mine, and I tried to derive all the meaning I could from that sad look she hung on me. My stomach churned.

"Cancer? What cancer? Since when?"

"Breast cancer. Since a few months ago."

"What?" I pulled my hair into a ponytail with great frustration and disbelief. "You had breast cancer for a few months, and you never told me?"

She only smiled at that.

"Why didn't you tell me, Mum?"

"I explained, I didn't want to worry you. You need to study."

An impossible mix of dread, fear, frustration, and anger took hold of me.

"Does Enav know?"

"I haven't told him yet."

I took my ponytail down and pulled it back up again. I didn't know what to do with my hands.

"So, what's the prognosis? Did they tell you?"

"It isn't good Jun, love."

"What do you mean?"

"Eighteen months at most, but probably no more than a year."

I could feel the tears prick my eyes.

"What treatment are they going to provide, Mum? Chemo? Are you going to have chemo?"

"They suggested it."

"And?"

"It's probably a little too late. They only offer a short treatment."

"Why only a short treatment?"

"Well, I imagine it's probably because it's become so expensive for them, with the health system under so much stress. You know, hunger is becoming a real issue in some places."

I jumped out of the chair and started walking nervously around the room. I didn't care about hunger; I cared about my Mum, and breast cancer.

"Short, long, who cares. If they suggested it, you need to take it, Mum! You don't know that it's too late, how would you know it's too late?"

"I'll do it, Jun. It's OK, I'll do it."

Was she serious, or was she just trying to shut me up?

"Mum..."

"Let me fix you something to eat," she said suddenly, and lifted herself out of bed, as if trying to prove to me she wasn't all dead yet. She was still in her nightie, and a bit smelly.

"Why don't you leave the cooking to me, Mum, and take a shower? It will make you feel better."

She looked at me, her body a little bent, looking slimmer and more brittle. I suddenly understood. There was no more joie de vivre in a home where someone who fears death lived. Someone who was depressed, and alone. I knew then that I'd have to drop out of law school and be with her.

I walked her to the shower and helped her inside. I took her nightgown and placed it in the washing machine. As she stood there, naked, under the warm water, I was horrified to see her sunken breasts, black and blue with all the tests and biopsies. She'd done them all alone, with no one to support her. It felt so wrong.

After the shower, Mum dressed in her old trainer pants and a t-shirt, and looked more cheerful, and somewhat restored, but I wondered if it was only a show that she'd put on for me. I cooked us lunch, then sat with her and ate in silence. I was in no mood to discuss silly, studently, inconsequential, social stuff. I didn't even want to talk about Crispin.

Not only did Mum need tending to, but the house was also in dire need of some care. Layers of unwiped sea sand covered the shelves and the kitchen benches. The floor needed sweeping and washing, and Mum's clothes piled up unwashed.

I changed her sheets, wiped the house clean, hung up the washing, then stepped outside with Johnny for a short relief walk. It was as much for me as it was for him. I stretched my back, expanded my chest, and drew in the sea air, inhaling deeply and exhaling slowly, like Mum showed me when I was little. The sea might have changed, but the sea air was still as salty, cool, and fresh as it'd always been. Johnny, careless and happy, ran around, barking at birds, picking up dry, old tree branches that the sea had pulled in, running around with a massive stick in his mouth. The simplest things in life made him happy. I used to be like that too.

I stayed overnight, tossing and turning in my childhood bed. I couldn't leave her on her own like that.

*

The next day, back at the university, I walked to the Dean's office and asked his assistant to schedule a personal meeting. She searched his calendar carefully, finally managing to find half an hour for us, two weeks away. I didn't realise deans were such busy people.

That evening I told Crispin.

"It's a mistake, Jun," he said. "You'll regret it."

"I'll regret it more if I leave Mum on her own with no one to be with her while she battles this cancer."

"What about your brother? He's not studying, so he can do it."

"I haven't told him yet."

"Why not? You need to tell him. Call him back home, it's not the right time for doing wooboo-jooboo in some retreat."

Crispin did not understand Enav's need for an emotional and spiritual outlet. It was foreign to him.

"I'm going to tell him, but it won't make a difference. Mum needs me, not him."

"How come?"

"I don't know, he won't be as attentive."

"Is he that selfish?"

"It's not what I meant!"

"Why, then? Why should you drop out of law school when he can just be home doing nothing?"

"Because Mum needs me. It's a bond thing. You wouldn't understand."

He sighed and shook his pretty head with that massive neck. "No, you're right, I don't understand. I think it's a mistake."

*

The Dean didn't understand either but was kind enough to agree to keep me on the books for a year, as if I was taking a sabbatical. I'd lose my hold of my dormitory room. It was a good compromise.

I finished my first year with an average of B-plus, even though my mind wasn't in my studies. As it ended, I packed up all my belongings and cleared out my dorm room. Teary goodbyes were said, and hugs given to all my friends, as we all disbanded for summer. I knew that even if I returned in a couple of years, they'd already be ahead of me, and it would not be the same.

The only one who stayed with me and wouldn't leave was Crispin. The first time he met Mum she had enthusiastically approved of him. Of course she did; no mother could withstand his charms. Only Enav wasn't impressed. "You can do better, Sis," he said.

I didn't know how he thought I could do better but assumed he was simply jealous of my companionship.

As I imagined, Enav tried to be helpful, but wasn't. He needed to be told to do things, instead of just seeing what needed to be done, and doing it. I constantly felt like the work manager who dictates tasks to their employees. "Load the washing, hang the washing, load the dishwasher, unload the dishwasher, sweep the floor, take Johnny out, give Johnny a bath, wipe the sand, you need to lift Mum's trinkets and wipe underneath not just around, do the shopping, look in the fridge and make a list, you didn't bring toilet paper, no, toilet paper isn't kept in the fridge but you should have checked in the broom cupboard anyway, I don't need to tell you everything, it's common sense." It was exhausting.

Mum only proved me right, as she always called for me when she needed help. I took her to her treatments, held her hand when they pricked her dwindled veins repeatedly to insert the IV line, then sat with her as she shrank into the deep chair, until she was sent home. I cleaned the pot she puked into, wiped her sweat, and her mouth, gave her the medication, helped her into bed, and when things got very bad, I helped her eat. I'd hold the spoon and bring it to her lips, then picked clean the bits that dribbled down her chin, just like she used to do when I was a little child. Roles had truly reversed.

*

"Maybe one day you'll need to feed me like that, Tui," I say, and smile at you, sleeping soundly in my arms. I kiss your warn cheek softly, inhaling your sweet scent.

I love you.

Thirty Four

The chemo didn't help, and Mum deteriorated quickly. Quicker than I'd hoped.

"It's time to talk about what happens when I'm gone," Mum said.

"Mum, please, there's plenty of time," Enav said, but he was wrong. There was only very little time left.

"I want you to sell the house if you can," Mum said weakly.

Enav and I exchanged looks. Who'd buy a house so close to the sea these days? So focused on her own decline, Mum wasn't aware of the steady environmental decline that happened in parallel. It seemed every month the sea was becoming wilder, higher, and closer.

"What if we can't sell, Mum?" I asked.

"Why couldn't you sell? A property by the beach has always been in high demand. It's hot property."

Again, Enav and I exchanged looks.

"Sell the house, sell everything. Use the money," she said. "Jun, I want you to go back to university. Finish your law degree. Enav, I want you to decide what you want to study and go for it, you've wasted enough time."

We sat in silence. Enav and I already knew that the house wouldn't sell, and no one would buy any of Mum's old stuff. The only thing we could possibly use was some of her jewellery, and that, even if we did decide to sell, which was unlikely, wouldn't cover my law degree or Enav's whatever degree. We knew that the house would be left as it was, to be eaten by the sea, like all the other houses on the beach.

We spent a lot of time sitting with her in silence. Once the medication kicked in, she would dive into an enhanced sleep, her breathing so shallow I'd keep checking for her pulse to see if she was still alive. When she was awake and more alert, she'd hate the silence, and would always start the conversation by saying, "So, tell me something new."

I'd search my brain to find something new, but there was nothing.

"I heard elephants have officially gone extinct," Enav said one time.

I threw him an angry look. What was the point, terrifying Mum in her condition with stories about how critical the situation outside had become?

"Elephants?" she wondered, her voice barely squeaking, "Extinct?"

"Uh, yes…" Enav said, hesitantly, obviously affected by my castigating look. "Koalas too."

I slapped his arm, making the word 'STOP' silently with my lips.

"What a shame," Mum said. "Us humans, we were never good caretakers of this planet." She then turned her head slowly to look at me. "Remember your toy elephant, Jun? When you were a little girl. You loved it so much, wouldn't leave the house without it. What was his name?"

"Rufus, it was a bear Mum, not an elephant. I still have him, in my room."

"Take him with you when I'm gone. Take him. You might have a child one day to give him to."

I knew I would, and here you are. Rufus is waiting for you in your crib, my beautiful Tui. He's yours now.

*

A week before Mum died, Crispin went down on one knee and asked me to marry him. I was taken by complete surprise. I was only twenty-two years old.

Twelve months before, I was a law student with dreams of a hotshot legal career. I had friends, I was independent, I had a home. Now, I had nothing. Mum was on her deathbed, I had no money, only Mum's few savings as inheritance, no future career, no friends.

Only Crispin, Enav and Johnny.

I loved Crispin, but I never saw myself marrying him. I didn't think he was the committing type, and I was in no hurry to attach myself to someone so permanently. But when he suddenly dropped on his knee and pulled out the ring, I was filled with some real joy, and a sudden sense of belonging. Crispin would be my home.

"Yes!" I gushed, as he placed the ring on my finger. He got back to his feet, looking so happy, and so handsome. He grabbed me and kissed me tenderly.

"Jun, babe. I'll take care of you. I'll look after you. You won't be alone, don't worry. I love you."

I always wondered if he only proposed because Mum was dying— that it was his sense of responsibility rather than deep desire to marry. Maybe Crispin didn't have big dreams, anyway. A career as a schoolteacher, a wife, a dog, and some kids, that's all he ever wanted.

*

Mum died peacefully in her bed. We held a small ceremony at the cemetery closest to the house, with only a few friends she had from church, some from work, and the Robinsons, the only neighbours left that still knew us. We could only afford a plain coffin for her; a simple gravestone marked her eternal resting place. The next day, Enav, Crispin and I went back to the house with black rubbish bags and threw out most of Mum's trinkets, keepsakes, her mishmash of souvenirs, and junk. Her whole life, in rubbish bins. Everything stood bare, devoid of personality. Only the faded wallpaper, darker where pictures used to hang, stood as testament to what was before, a happy little place.

"Are you sure you wouldn't like to stay here?" Crispin asked Enav.

"Heck, no," Enav replied with a tone of revulsion that was a tad too strong.

"It's rent-free," Crispin insisted.

"I don't want to stay here," Enav said, turning his back to Crispin, indicating the conversation was over.

I sort of understood Enav's vehement resistance to living in Mum's house. Living there, with the old memories, in a world that was fast changing, when everything that was good about that house was gone and buried, would be completely depressing. We couldn't resurrect our childhood, or our happiness, or those days of carefreeness. The house stood as a living tombstone to a life we couldn't get back. Best to leave it be.

I packed my stuff, made sure Tui's letter was in my pocket, and that Rufus the bear and Mum's few pieces of jewellery were in my bag. The old washing machine went with Enav to his new rented flat. The dishwasher broke even before Mum had passed. Crispin and I took Johnny and moved in together.

*

"Your dad and I wed in a small ceremony, at the church where Mum used to go. A few of your dad's cousins came, and his friends from university, and from his college rugby club days. On my side, there was only Uncle Enav, who looked as if he had swallowed a lemon, the whole time."

I chuckle at the thought.

"Oh, and Johnny was there, Tui. You'd have loved him. He most probably was the life of the party."

I laugh at the memory of Johnny bouncing and licking everyone and anyone, ripping my simple wedding dress at the hem.

"I miss him, Tui," I say, softly running my finger over her soft, warm cheek. "I miss Johnny."

Then, sighing, I add, "I miss Uncle Enav, too. He's sort of disappeared; you know. I miss Mum. I miss a lot of things."

There's an ache in my chest, and the tears start streaming down my face.

"Hey, what's the matter, Jun?" Crispin asks, as he walks into the room, looking worried.

"Oh, nothing. I've been sharing some old memories with Tui, that's all."

"So, why the tears? Are these sad memories?"

"Oh no, that's nothing. It's just the hormones talking."

FIVE

YEARS

EARLIER:

2033

Thirty Five

I walk into the house, and I just know that Mum has been made upset by something she must have heard on the news. She's standing over the stove, mumbling to herself, stirring the innocent rice in the pot so ferociously, it looks like she's trying to make it fly.

"What's up, Mum?" I say as I lightly kiss her cheek. "Who's upset you this time?"

"Oh, that stupid prime minister, I tell you!" she grumbles, shaking her head. "Why are all our politicians always so useless, huh, Juni? Why?"

"I don't know. Why aren't you one? You could have been a good politician."

"Nah," she mutters, "give me a break."

She turns off the cooker and covers the pot. "Short-sighted, corrupt imbeciles! The lot of them. What would I be doing with that bunch?"

I smile. She's funny when she's upset.

"So, what did they do this time?" I ask her.

"What did they do? It's what they didn't do! Not them, and not the imbecile before them, and not the imbecile before the imbecile before them. They didn't do shit!"

"Mum!" I giggle, surprised at Mum's language. She rarely used bad words. She must have been made terribly unhappy. "What happened?"

"Didn't you hear? Now they say that all those plans to reduce emissions, so that temperatures don't go above two degrees— remember that, Juni? Over a decade ago it was—well, it's all been some stinky fudge! Now they're saying that we should have gone under one point five, and even that would have been too little too late. It's all too late! Now, suddenly, this imbecile is saying we need to transition to a plant-based economy, blah, blah, blah!"

She wipes her forehead with the sweat that pools there from all the stirring.

"Where were you ten years ago, imbecile number four? Huh? Kissing arses and spreading promises, like some… STD!"

"Mum!" I giggle again.

"And of course, as per usual, all the animal farmers are in uproar. They're going to lose their livelihood and all that. Well, sure, where was the government when we demanded programmes and funding to support farmers to transition and diversify? Nothing, they did nothing! Ghaaa! I'm so cross!"

"I can see that, Mum. But this isn't new, right? It's been going on for a while. I remember talks about moving to a plant-based economy when I was a kid."

"Well, yes. We kept trying to get the government to endorse it! We wanted them to do something, to save us, to save you—your generation, and your children's generation, and all the animals too. But no, they just had to kiss more arses, you know."

Mum sighs.

"It's all going to turn to custard, Juni. All of it. To say now that 'we need to transition', it's too late!" She exhales loudly, looking defeated. "It's too late."

Johnny runs into the kitchen, barking and jumping, covered in sand and wet with seawater. Enav is right behind him.

"Hey, Sis," he says, as he hangs Johnny's leash on the hook by the door. "I hear you got into law school! Congratulations!" He comes over and gives me a clumsy hug.

"Thanks," I say with a smile. I'm really proud of myself. I worked hard to get into Law School.

"Oh yes, Juni, I didn't congratulate you yet," Mum shakes her gloominess off and hunches over to kiss my cheek. "I baked your favourite apple cake, and there's beer in the fridge."

I shriek with joy.

"But first let's have something to eat. I made some rice and some vegetable curry."

"You mean the rice that you were trying to assassinate just before?" I ask, chuckling.

"It lived. Let me plate some for you. We can have the cake later. Enav! Come, sit."

"OK, but the beer now," I say, as I fetch three beer bottles from the fridge, a bottle opener from the drawer, and one glass from the cupboard. Only Mum uses a glass for her beer. Enav and I drink straight from the bottle.

"Take your foot off the chair," Mum reprimands my favourite position. "And why do you drink from the bottle? We have more glasses."

"Mum, every time the same thing. I prefer it this way."

"People might think I raised you like a hooligan," Mum mutters.

"No, they won't," I say and wink at her.

She chuckles.

Johnny squeezes himself between us, below the small dining table, then sticks his head out from underneath, lifting the hem of the tablecloth as he does, salivating over my legs. I pick a little rice from my plate and let him lick it off my hand.

"That's why he's spoiled," Mum says.

"As if you don't do it!" I laugh.

"You do it too, Mum," Enav agrees. We all laugh.

"Well yeah, because he learned how to beg. He learned it from you," Mum says in an apologetic tone, and smiles.

"You spoil him the most, Mum," Enav says as he takes another sip from his beer. "Admit it!"

"No."

"Yes, you do! He sleeps on your bed!"

"Because he chewed his own bed."

Enav and I laugh. "Sure, sure."

We love this family time banter. Enav and I always pair up and gang up on Mum. That's the routine. It's innocent and not offensive. Mum likes it too. She's almost always the one who starts it.

Johnny seems to know the fuss is all about him, as he rotates between us, tail wagging under the table, asking for—and receiving—more rice to lick.

*

After lunch, I decide to go for a walk on the beach with Johnny. It's been quite hot for a long time now, but here, the sea breeze cools you down. The waves are more aggressive nowadays though, compared to how it was when I was a child. They reach further, harder, with some sense of vengeance, as if trying to grab more with them, when they withdraw.

Johnny runs and barks at the few birds. He's such a funny dog. Soon we'll reach the point where I found him, only five years ago. *Five years?* It seems so much more.

I was fourteen, going on fifteen, on the beach after school, as usual, looking for a shaded spot to sit and read my book. I think it was 'Lord of the Flies'. Enav wasn't with me. He was already nineteen then, and was pretending to be looking for a job, or for some other motivating incentives to get himself out of the house and come back late. It was doing Mum's head in. He was so unfocussed, so clueless, so lacking ambition. He'd start every week with a new idea of what to do with himself, follow it up a little, then end the week with the certainty that it wasn't for him after all. Meanwhile he randomly worked, earning below minimum wage, having very few friends, if any.

As I was contemplating where to sit with my book, I saw this ball of wet, black fur running towards me. He came to me, wagging his tail, sniffing me, and smiling. Yes, smiling.

"Hello!" I said. "Who are you?"

I looked for a collar, but he had none. I stretched my neck to see if there was a person coming up behind him, calling for him, but there was no one.

The fur ball was panting hard, repeatedly licking his lips.

"Are you thirsty, my friend?" I asked.

"Wait, are you a boy or a girl?"

I leaned and checked the dog's behind.

"A boy!"

He seemed to be very happy with that tone of voice.

"Come boy, I'll give you something to drink. Come!"

He didn't need much encouragement, following me home, bouncing and wagging his tail. I took the salad bowl that was drying from lunch, filled it with water and placed it on the floor. The dog drank, and drank, and drank, leaving me astounded. He nearly drank the bowl dry.

"Wow…" I sighed. "You must be hungry too, eh?"

He was. I made him a sandwich, with some olive oil spread and tofu. He gobbled it in a single bite. So, I made him more. By the time he gobbled the third, Mum walked in, back from work, clearly tired and unimpressed.

"What's going on here? Who's this?"

"It's, um, it's… Johnny."

"Johnny? Where did he come from?"

"I think someone left him on the beach."

"Well, someone might be coming back to the beach to look for him."

"No, he was there a while, on his own. He was so thirsty, look, he drank the whole bowl!"

"Is this the salad bowl?" Mum was horrified.

"Don't worry, I'll wash it."

"Wash it? Jun, this isn't our dog. He can't stay here."

"He has no home. Someone left him alone on the beach. I'm not returning him."

"He can't stay here!"

"Why not? I'll look after him."

"Of course, you would, and who will pick up his poop? And who will pay for the food he eats? And who will pay for the vet bills he might have? You? Or your successful brother?"

"I'll chip in. I can take a summer job. I'll clean up after him."

"Jun, he doesn't belong here. Don't leave him here because I'm just going to throw him out!"

"He has nowhere else to go, Mum. You're the one who always keeps talking about compassion and loving the animals as if they were our kin, never hurting them, never treating them like they're objects rather than individuals. Well—here is an abandoned dog. He is an individual, not an object. He is alone. He is afraid. He is hungry and thirsty. We need to exercise that compassion. Now is the time."

Mum stared at me, half smiling, rubbing her neck.

I stood there, waiting to continue my onslaught of good reasons to keep the dog, while Johnny just stood there, looking at Mum, wagging his tail.

"On one condition, Juni. First, we take him to the vet, see if he belongs to someone. Maybe he ran away. They can check for that little chip with the details. Then we'll see."

I jumped and hugged Mum, delighted.

Mum patted Johnny on his head, then went to her bedroom to change out of her working clothes. "You should be a lawyer," she threw behind her back, and closed her bedroom door.

*

The next day, we took Johnny to the vet.

It turned out Johnny was microchipped. There was a phone number to call on his registration data.

My spirit fell. He did have an owner. He was simply lost, not abandoned.

The vet nurse went to the back room and dialled the number, but it was disconnected. She then searched up the number on some database, found a link to a possible owner, and called the second number. I didn't want it to be a success, but a man answered. From the tone of the conversation, it seemed the nurse was becoming very frustrated.

We'd been waiting a while before she returned.

"OK, so this is Isaac. He's three years old."

"Isaac?"

"Yes. He has an owner, but the owner doesn't want him. You might be right in thinking that Isaac was abandoned deliberately."

"See?" I said to Mum.

"I can transfer the ownership to you if you want him. Isaac needs to be checked, but he looks healthy."

"What if we don't take him?" Mum asked.

"Well, then he'll stay here, and we'll try to find him a new home."

"And if you fail?" Mum kept probing.

"That hardly ever happens," the vet nurse said, "but if no new home is found, we'll need to transfer him to the pound."

"To be killed?"

This question made the vet nurse clearly uncomfortable. "Well, sometimes dogs do have to be euthanised."

I stared harshly at Mum. I knew she passionately hated the word 'euthanised'. It was a wishy-washy, conscience-soothing, cover-up word for killing, she'd always say. There was no way we were leaving without Isaac. No, not 'Isaac'. What sort of a name was that for a dog? Without Johnny.

Mum said nothing for a while.

"So, what would you like to do?" the vet nurse asked.

Mum looked at the vet nurse, then looked at me, then at Johnny. She rubbed her neck and sighed.

"OK, yes. We'll take him."

FIVE
YEARS
EARLIER:
2028

Thirty Six

I wake up to Mum and Enav arguing again. Mum is frustrated with Enav's inability to decide what he wants to study, or be, or create, or look for.

"What's the rush? Why are you pushing me like that?" Enav keeps saying.

"I don't push you enough, that's the problem. I never pushed you. Now you're drifting, like a leaf without a place to land."

"I don't need to be pushed! And I'm not a leaf! I need the freedom to find my purpose by myself, in my own time! Why are you nagging me?"

"I'm not nagging. I need to go to work. If you're doing nothing, at least clean the house, tidy up, help out."

"I always help."

"You never help. Why don't you take Juni to school today, eh? That will help."

"I can do that."

"OK. And make her breakfast."

I wait until I hear Mum leaving, before I slowly open my bedroom door.

"What was all that about?" I ask, rubbing my face, and stifling a yawn.

"Eh, Mum's on my case again," Enav says, placing two pieces of my favourite grainy bread in the toaster. "What d'ya want on your toast?"

"Nut spread, the one without palm oil—not that one, it's the green one—and Vegemite. What is your case?"

"My case you know, is that I need to decide what to do when I grow up," he says as he grabs the nut spread out of the fridge, then takes the Vegemite from the pantry. "Remind me what you drink in the morning? You're too young for coffee, eh?"

"Oat milk chocolate drink," I reply. "I thought you wanted to be an opera singer."

Enav chuckles.

"What?" I ask.

"I was never good at singing," he says. "It was just a silly dream."

"But you can get better, can't you? If you go to, I don't know, opera school or something. I'm sure they have schools where you can learn it? Get better?"

"Nah, I don't think so," he says, as he places the toast on a plate, applies the nut spread generously, then a thin layer of the Vegemite. "You probably need to start when you're very young, you know, like ballet and stuff."

He puts the plate in front of me as I sit at the dining table, then pours the oat milk chocolate drink into a tall glass for me.

"What are you going to do, then?" I ask, as I bite into the warm toast, enjoying the crunchiness of the bread, the saltiness with the slight tanginess of the Vegemite spread. I wash it down with the sweetness of the oat milk.

"I don't know. That's the whole problem, isn't it? I thought maybe I could be a marine biologist."

"What's that?"

"It's a biologist that specialises in marine life."

"What do they do?"

"I don't know, research?"

"So, you want to be a researcher?"

"Jeez, are you trying to be like Mum, with all these interrogations?"

"No," I say as I brush toast crumbs from my pyjamas, "I don't care what you're going to be, I'm just curious. I don't know what a marine biologist does."

"Well, I explained it. It's someone that researches marine life, sea life."

"OK. Are you taking me to school today?"

"Yes, so get ready, we should be leaving soon."

*

I'm not particularly keen on school. I'm not the most popular girl. I find most girls my age extremely shallow, spending most of their time on screens, imitating looks they've been told by famous people they should have, making themselves seem much more available and mature than they are, quantifying success by the number of people liking them on various social applications. I don't feel like I'm part of that. I don't want to be part of that.

I have one friend. Her name is Aisha and she's not in my class. We became friends the day I wore my 'Friends Not Food' T-shirt to school. Mum bought me that T-shirt. The back said, 'Close all slaughterhouses by twenty twenty-five,' but it was already twenty twenty-seven when I wore it, and that still didn't happen. Mum said it had to happen before twenty thirty or we were all doomed, not only the poor, defenceless animals, but all of humanity.

"I like your shirt," Aisha said on the lunch break, only I didn't know her name then.

"Thanks," I answered, with a bit of suspicion. Sometimes people said they liked the things I cared about, only to mock me about it later.

"Can I sit here?" she asked, pointing at the bench space next to me.

"Sure."

She looked so lovely and chic, with her shiny, sleek, long brown hair worn loose, just one hair clip to remove the glossy veil from her face. Her glasses were so 'now' as if chosen straight from a catalogue, and her face was tanned and so healthy-looking, it put me and all the hours I spent on the beach to shame.

She took out her sandwich. I always felt very uncomfortable when people did it next to me. I hated watching and smelling people eat dead animals in their bread. But Aisha's bread had only avocado and slices of tomatoes.

"What are you having?" she asked.

"Jam."

We sat there together, in silence.

"Do you go to vigils?" Aisha asked suddenly.

"To where?"

"Vigils. There's a group of people holding vigils sometimes, outside the slaughterhouse. It's like small, peaceful protests, I guess. I just thought, you know, because of your shirt."

"No, I never went there. Maybe my Mum has. She does all that stuff."

"Good on her."

"Yeah."

"My name is Aisha."

"I'm Juniper."

"I can see you have your book out, I've got a book too. Do you mind if we read together?"

"I don't mind."

"Cool."

*

We became best friends that very day. We had so much in common, it was meant to be. She was also raised by a single mother, with a sister, five years older than her. We were both raised to love animals and not hurt them, certainly never to eat them. We loved books and could discuss them endlessly, excitedly. And neither of us was trying desperately to make ourselves look older, or sexier, as many of the other girls were.

After school, we walked home together. Aisha didn't live by the beach, but close to the centre of our little town. She was ecstatic that first time, when she found out my home was right by the sea.

"You've got to be kidding me!' she shouted. 'That's like, my dream home!'"

I smiled. "Want to come over?"

"Yeah-yuh! Totally!"

We stopped first at Aisha's house, to let her mum know she was coming home with me. Her mum was a designer of some kind, working in a studio at their house. I walked in after Aisha, impressed with the vast space of the house, the whiteness of the walls, the generous windows, the modern artwork everywhere. I was a little embarrassed to bring Aisha to my house after being at hers.

Before we left, Aisha poured us some cold water, then pressed a handle on the front of the fridge that made it spit ice cubes out. She dunked a few in my glass. That was a very impressive trick. When the fridge at my house managed to close properly with the first try, that was considered a success.

But Aisha loved my house. She loved mum's random trinkets and all the weird stuff we had on display. She loved the beach, tossing off our shoes on the front porch then running to the warm sand. Putting our feet in the cold water, running away, squealing, as the waves came near.

After that, she came home with me almost every day after school. Mum would come home to find Aisha and me still on the beach, sometimes talking, sometimes reading together, in silence. She'd make us a small plate of snacks and bring it to us. We'd sit, eating our grapes, or rice crackers, or pretzels, inhaling the sea air, watching the sun getting ready to dive into the horizon.

"You're so bloody lucky," Aisha would say.

"Your house is nice too."

"Nothing like this."

*

I never stayed at her house, the way she stayed at mine. I didn't know why Aisha didn't like being home, but she never asked me to come to her place, not even once, for a change.

"My Mum's always busy," she said, "especially now with her new boyfriend."

"Your mum's got a boyfriend?"

"Yeah. I don't really like him though."

"How come?"

"I don't' know. It's a feeling."

One time we stopped at Aisha's house on the way to mine, only to pick up Aisha's book which she forgot to bring with her that day. We walked into the house to hear her mum and the boyfriend moaning in the bedroom.

Aisha made a puking gesture, got her book, and grabbed my hand to leave.

"Can you believe the grossness?" she said when we were outside. "They're at it all the time. It's disgusting."

"Well, at least she's with someone who loves her," I said.

"This isn't love, Juniper. This is lust. They're like, eating each other all the time. It's embarrassing."

"She doesn't love him?"

"I don't know. I don't care," Aisha said. "It would be nice if she remembered she had kids, every now and then, know what I'm saying?"

I didn't. My Mum never forgot she had kids. She was always there. Too much, according to Enav.

"Maybe your mum would like to adopt me?" Aisha chuckled, but it was a sad chuckle. Forced.

I didn't know what to say to that.

*

Enav leaves me at the school gate, and I walk in. I look for Aisha at the front yard, but she isn't there. I put my bag in my locker, then go look for her. She's not in her classroom, not on the field, not in the gym. Strange. The bell rings, creating a stampede of crazed students, running everywhere, bumping into each other as they race each other to their classrooms. I can't see Aisha anywhere.

In the break I sit alone, eating my sandwich, reading my book. Aisha isn't there.

After school I walk home, passing Aisha's home on my way. I must check what happened to her today. I open the wooden gate and ring the bell. I can hear the sound of the 'ding-dong' echoing inside, but the door remains shut. I knock, but it isn't answered.

Concerned, I turn away and leave through the wooden gate. Something is definitely off.

Thirty Seven

"Where have you been?" I shout at Aisha. She's been away, off the radar, out of reach, not a peep, for over a week. "It's like you evaporated!"

"Yeah, pretty much," Aisha sighs. She seems withdrawn. "Sorry."

"What happened?" I ask. "I was so worried!"

For the first time, I see tears in Aisha's eyes, and they start rolling down her face, and drip to the floor. She always seemed so tough; suddenly she's fragile and I'm terrified by it.

"Sorry," she says as she starts weeping, wiping her nose on the back of her arm. She leans into me, and I hug her.

"What's going on?" I ask.

"Mum's boyfriend, that useless arse," Aisha cries softly, "he left her."

"I thought that was a good thing?"

"Yes, a great thing, if you ask me. But Mum went mental."

I wasn't sure where that story was going. Aisha never liked the guy, so if he'd left, her mum might be sad for a while, then it would all be good again, surely.

"She tried to kill herself, Juniper. Over that stupid, stupid, piece-of-shit of a man. She tried to kill herself," Aisha cries.

I tighten my arms around her, sensing my friend is broken. Why would Aisha's Mum do something so irrational, so horrible like that?

"Is your mum OK?"

"Yes, she's home now," Aisha straightens herself, out of my arms, rubbing her nose clean. "I had to go to my Nana for a while. It was all a bit crazy, I'm sorry. I found her, you know, in the tub."

She takes a tissue out of her pocket and wipes her nose. "All the blood and shit. So, they put all the psychologists and all the social workers and stuff on me. It was... a mess. Sorry I wasn't in touch."

"It's all right," I say, still in complete shock.

"I'm probably going to move permanently to my nana's," she says, and even though everything she'd told me was horrifying, her leaving was the hardest news to swallow.

"Why? Why would you leave?"

"Because my mum is still weak, and she needs medical help, and she's not capable of functioning at this point in time. She might be alive but she's like, she's like dead, you know?"

I nod, but I find it very hard to understand.

"So, when will you know?"

"When will I know what?"

"That you're going to live with your nan?"

"Oh, I already know. I'm definitely going. Today. I only came to say goodbye."

I'm so disappointed to hear that. From how she said it, I thought moving away was an option, not a certainty. Suddenly, the truth sinks in, that I might not see her again. She was my best friend. My only friend.

"Will you have time to come to the beach today after school, before you go?"

"No, sorry. I'm probably not even staying the full day. My nan is packing up my stuff, she'll come to pick me up in an hour or so. I just came to say goodbye."

My heart drops. She hasn't left yet, and already I feel so lonely. I mean, I was lonely before, but I didn't really know any better. This past year, with Aisha, I've been shown the excitement of having a close friend. Being lonely now would be a hundred times worse than before.

"I'm really sorry, Juniper," Aisha says, suddenly crying again, as she hugs me so tightly, I nearly choke. "You were my bestest friend ever. I'm really going to miss you," she cries.

"Me too."

The bell rings and mayhem erupts, with students running amok everywhere. Aisha and I are still hugging, knowing that it's the last time, it's the final hug.

"You should go," Aisha says, and she lets go of me.

Reluctantly I walk away towards my classroom. I turn back only to wave, feebly. She's already gone.

*

My sadness is so heavy, I feel it is almost a real, physical weight that I'm carrying around me.

I walk home, past Aisha's old house. It seems empty. I wish she'd come back. Why would her mother act in this way? Doing something so horrid? I bet she didn't even know that her actions would impact people who were completely outside of her immediate circle, people like me. But I was impacted by it. My life would now completely change. I'd need to retune and readjust my joie de vivre again, to find my happiness again, to reach my balance by myself.

The more I thought of it, the more it made me angry. To do something so extreme because of some guy. I'd never do that. Never. Not for no man. Not ever.

*

Even the beach seems gloomy without Aisha. I toss my shoes at the front door, but I don't run out to the sand, I just grab my book and walk slowly. It's very hot. I don't feel like putting my feet in the water. I just want to find some shade where I can sit and read my book in peace. Aisha's departure out of my life has been so sudden, I feel as if she died. I'm grieving her loss. I wonder if I'll ever have another friend like her. If I'll ever have another friend at all. Maybe that's my destiny, to be lonely.

I'm so sunk in my own sadness that I must be hallucinating, because I swear, I can see a black, wet, fluffball on the beach, running towards me.

FIVE

YEARS

EARLIER:

2023

Thirty Eight

Last week was my birthday. I turned nine years old. Mum suggested I invite some friends from school to celebrate together, but it was a bit difficult. I have no friends. Not really. I mean, there's Bethany and Lila who play with me during the big break, sometimes, but mostly they don't. Mostly, I walk aimlessly around the sports field, or find a quiet corner to read a book.

I think Mum took it to heart. Maybe a little too much, since she's organised a street party for me, inviting all the people from the neighbouring houses on the beach. People we couldn't name, hardly knew, and had rarely met before.

"Why are you inviting the neighbours?" I asked.

"We need to have a party," Mum explained, "so why not have a neighbourhood potluck?"

"But we don't know any of them."

"A great opportunity to get to know them, don't you think?" Mum answered.

Mum created the invites on the old computer, and since we didn't have a printer at home, she printed them at her workplace. They had a colourful image of a golden, sunny beach, that looked more like a fancy island holiday destination than the rugged beach we lived by. The invites also said, 'Bring no gifts, and only plant-based food'.

"You just made sure nobody will come," Enav said, reading the invite.

"How come?" Mum asked, looking a little offended.

"They'll see only plant-based food and run," Enav chuckled.

"Have faith," Mum smiled.

She's been outside, by the front gate, with Enav, since ten in the morning, setting up the portable gazebo, cleaning and readying the barbecue grill, filling a large bucket with dry ice for the beer, and organising the folding picnic table and chairs. She enjoys all this fussing around. I think this party is more for her, really, than it is for me. If it was up to me, I'd just be spending the day on the beach with Enav, and that would've been good enough.

I can hear voices from outside, so I guess some neighbours did show up. Enav must be impressed.

"Juniper! Come out!" Enav is shouting through the front door. "We have guests!"

As if they'd care if I was there or not.

I walk out. There are four people I don't think I've seen before. They seem to be two couples, one closer to Mum's age, one a bit older.

"And this is Juniper, who had her birthday last week," Mum says, as she grabs me to her in a forced hug, with her right-hand combing through my hair with her fingers, trying to get it to look less messy.

"Hi," I say, to no one specifically.

"Hi," the four of them answer together, reminding me of our ridiculous school choir.

"These are the Reids." Mum points out the two older people, who smile at me. They are both wearing so much sunscreen, their faces are nearly white. I have to giggle.

"And these are the Robinsons," Mum adds, as she indicates the younger couple.

"Hi," I say again.

"Happy birthday," says Mr Reid, smiling, looking a bit scary with his white face and big teeth.

"Thanks."

"How old are you, deary?" asks Mrs Reid.

"Nine."

"Oh, great age," she replies.

I shrug.

"What school do you go to?" asks Mrs Robinson, who has no sunscreen, but a lot of make-up instead.

"Queen Elizabeth Primary."

"Oh, I believe my niece goes there," Mrs Robinson says. "Felicia Mortimer, do you know her?"

I shake my head. Never heard of any Felicia Mortimer.

"She might be a little younger than you, actually," Mrs Robinson adds.

I wonder how much longer this torture is going to take before Mum is happy enough to let me go back inside.

Another couple is making their way towards us from further down the beach, smiling widely and waving.

"Hello, hi, hi, hello," the woman, her arms covered in noisy bangles, says, as they get near. The man, a big, hairy guy, adds six bottles of beer to the ice bucket, and places down a tray of what looks very much like real diced animals shaped into what looks like a bunch of boys' willies.

"Oh," Mum inhales. "Oh, are these plant-based?"

"They ate plenty of plants when they were alive, I'm sure!" the man cackles, his voice booming.

"Oh, sorry, we're only plant-based," Mum says quickly. "I hope you don't mind. It said so on the invite."

"Oh, Vera didn't tell me. Vera!" the man shouts to the woman who came with him. "You didn't tell me not to bring meat, you said it was a barbie!"

The woman, who must be Vera, smiles meekly. "Sorry, I wasn't sure what you meant by plant-based, because you said it was a barbecue…"

"No matter, we have loads of food," Mum says. "Here, you can take it back." She quickly wraps the animal flesh and hands it to the man. He takes it and walks back home. I wonder if he'll come back.

But Vera stays with us, still smiling meekly.

"We were surprised at the variety of plant-based sausages we found at the supermarket," Mr Robinson says. "I never knew there were so many."

"Times are really changing, aren't they," Mrs Reid agrees. "Robert and I are doing Meat Free Mondays at the moment. For the planet."

I look at Mum. Her face seems like she's swallowed a lemon. I bet she's dying to tell them that giving up meat a single day per week isn't enough, but she's promised Enav not to cause a scene, and is focussed on the vegan patties on the grill.

Vera's man comes back, this time with a tinned cake, the kind you buy ready-made at the supermarket. Mum accepts it with a smile, and quickly reads the ingredients list on the back before she approves it.

The food smells good, so I decide to stay until after I eat.

"How long have you been living here?" Mrs Robinson asks Mum.

"Fifteen years," Mum says.

"Fifteen! Wow. We've been here four years," Mrs Robinson replies, to a question she wasn't asked. "It's so beautiful here, so quiet."

She looks around, then adds, "I can't believe it's only now that we're getting together, us all. Eh? Thank you for organising this."

Mum smiles and nods.

"We're only renting," Vera's man says. "I wouldn't have bought our house."

"How come?" Mr Reid asks.

"It's not a good investment to buy beach property these days," Vera's man says. "Climate change will impact this market."

"Nonsense," Mr Reid says. "What impact?"

"Rising sea levels," Vera's man says.

Mr Reid laughs. "We're not in bloody—what's the name of the place—Tuvalu!"

Vera hands her man another beer. I think he's already had two.

Mr Reid doesn't seem to like Vera's man very much, as he's arguing with him about beach lifestyles and all sorts of things I don't really understand. Grown-ups can be so strange sometimes.

"Want to split to the beach?" Enav whispers in my ear.

I nod so hard my neck hurts.

"Mum, can we go to the beach?" Enav asks.

"Eat first," Mum commands.

"Can we take our plates to the beach?" he asks.

"Please Mum! Please!" I add to his begging.

"OK," Mum says, and hands us two plates loaded with vegan sausages, patties, baked potatoes, and grilled mushrooms.

We grab the plates, and run behind the house, to the beach.

"Let's make a deal," Enav says.

"What's the deal?" I ask.

"We don't go back until that potluck is over."

"Deal!"

Thirty Nine

It's such a beautiful day! I love it when summer starts. Enav and I can play on the beach all day long, no school to interrupt us, no homework or any of that stuff. I deliberately leave the curtains drawn open overnight, so that I can wake up early, before seven, sometimes before even six! I wait for Mum to wake up and fix me breakfast, before she goes to work, and then, if Enav is still sleeping—because he's fourteen, and a teenager, and such a sleepy head—I wake him. Well, I try to wake him, because sometimes he just rolls over to the other side and keeps on sleeping.

I have to wait for Enav before I go to the beach, because Mum won't allow me to go on my own; she says I'm too young, and you don't know who else might be on the beach. I don't think Mum has any reason to worry, because I never see anyone else out there, it's always just Enav and me. But I do as she says, because I don't want to get her upset. Also because, with my luck, the one time I actually go on my own, something WILL happen. So, I wait for Enav to wake up, and I make a lot of noise in the house, slamming doors, turning on the radio, things like that, until Sleeping Beauty finally appears.

When Enav is awake and finally up, he makes himself some breakfast, then goes to brush his teeth, and everything drags on, and on, until finally he's ready to go out to the beach with me. On days when he says he doesn't feel like going, I'll be nagging and nagging and nagging him so much, he'll go just to keep me quiet.

Today he's up and ready earlier than usual, maybe because I sneaked into his bedroom last night and opened his curtains, so that he'd be woken by early light. It also helped that it's Saturday, and Mum isn't going to work, so breakfast is ready nice and early.

Enav and I are at the beach, hopping between rocks, looking for hermit crabs. We love watching them peek out from the sand, between rocks, and run over to hide with the shells they use as cover. They're funny. Sometimes we find fish, stuck in small pools that form between the rocks, especially at low tide, and we help them back to sea. But in the past two years we've been noticing we can find fewer hermit crabs and fewer fish. There's definitely a change in the number of living things that we can see in the water.

When we told Mum about it a few months ago, she didn't seem surprised. Her friend, a diver who goes diving in all sorts of exotic places in the Pacific Ocean, had told her that he finds fewer and fewer fish, and that coral reefs have been steadily bleaching. I asked Mum what it means, and she said it means that the corals are dying and losing all their colour and beauty, and the fish die with it. Mum said that the sea was dying because humans have been too greedy for too long. I wasn't a hundred percent sure what she meant by that, so instead of asking her, I ask Enav.

"It's climate change," he says. "The coral reefs are bleaching because the temperature of the ocean is changing. And there's also the problem of overfishing," Enav explains.

"Overfishing? What's that?"

"It's when people come with their huge trawlers, they throw massive nets into the ocean, and bring up a ginormous haul of fish, turtles, dolphins, stingrays, sharks, whatever. It's a total destruction of complete ecosystems."

"Why do people do that?" I ask, even though I'm only half certain that I'm correctly guessing what ecosystem means.

"For money."

I know from Mum, that whenever people do something just for the money, just for themselves, without thinking of what it does to others, it could be pretty bad.

"But Enav, aren't there lots of fish in the ocean?" I ask, trying to find a bit of hope to hang onto.

"Nah, not enough," Enav replies. "People take too much, it's all take, take, take. Life in the ocean doesn't have enough time to respond and replace the dead and destroyed with new lives."

I gasp. It sounds quite hopeless.

"Because of that," Enav continues, "we lose the diversity of sea creatures who are dependent on each other for survival, so it all collapses, like dominoes. You know how dominos fall, one on top of the other?"

I nod.

"Well, eventually, after all this destruction and collapsing, all life in the ocean will go extinct. I read somewhere that this is expected in twenty forty-eight, and that's a big worry, because when the sea dies, humans will die too," Enav says.

"How come?" I ask, as I try to quickly calculate how much time I have left, but I'm not very strong with math.

"Because of all the phytoplankton."

"Phyto…?"

"Plankton. They're like tiny, teeny, small critters. They help take the dangerous gas from the air, called carbon dioxide, and release oxygen, which is the good gas that we breathe."

"Wow." Enav knows so much interesting stuff. I wonder if I'll know quite as much when I'm fourteen.

"Yeah. Did you know, most of the oxygen we breathe comes from the ocean? It's like an oxygen machine."

"I didn't know that." I feel like I know absolutely nothing.

"But if life in the sea collapses, there will be no more phytoplankton, and no more oxygen machine. Humans can't live without oxygen."

"What can we do?" I ask in alarm.

"First, we must fight overfishing, and second, we must fight climate change. Do you know what 'climate change' actually means?"

"Yeah, Mum talks about it."

"What do you know?"

"It's um…that our planet becomes warm because of the pollution in the atmosphere?" I say, suddenly unsure.

"Yeah, not bad, Sis, you're not far off," Enav replies, and I smile proudly. "You're talking about the 'Greenhouse Effect', which is happening because of all the bad gasses. The important thing you should know is, that it doesn't simply mean we'll just get hotter. It means that because of climate change, the weather starts behaving differently, wildly, dangerously. Icebergs melt, the water temperature changes, ecosystems collapse, everything goes bonkers."

"So, it's dangerous?" I ask, feeling scared.

"Yes."

"What can we do to fight climate change then?"

"Well, the one thing people should be doing, but most aren't doing yet, is stop eating animals."

"*We* don't!"

"No, we don't. But most people still do. It's horrible. Eating animals pollutes the soil, the water, and the atmosphere. It's one of the worst polluters. It also uses so much land, that we lose biodiversity."

"Bio… diver?"

"Biodiversity. It means a lot of different types of plants and wildlife are destroyed forever. Just like with the ocean, same thing on land."

"So why don't people stop doing it?"

"Because people don't like change."

"That's stupid!"

"I know, but that's how lots of people are. Change makes them afraid for some reason. Also, animal agriculture is a huge business that makes a lot of money."

Again, this thing with money. I get the feeling all the evil in the world is caused by people's love for it.

"Can't they make money by doing other things?" I ask.

"I'm sure they can. With some help from the government, maybe."

I can tell Enav is all worked up now, as his speech becomes faster.

"Did you know, last year there was this big meeting of representatives from countries all around the world, to discuss what to do about climate change," he says.

I'm filled with sudden hope. I bet they're going to fix it!

"So, all these people met in Egypt, and do you know what they were given to eat?" Enav asks, his voice raised.

"Crispy Tofu?"

"No! Meat! Steak and fish!" he shouts.

"Maybe they didn't know?" I try.

Enav laughs.

"They know. Government officials meet to talk about climate change, so it looks like they're trying, but they're not. Nothing is being done. It's called greenwashing."

It makes no sense to me.

"The one thing that can help us is if all nations change to plant-based living, but that won't happen. D'you know, just a few months ago a report by the big, international body for climate change, called the IPCC…"

Enav stresses each letter, Eye-Pee-Cee-Cee, like each of them annoys him individually-

"…was released, and they were convinced, or maybe bullied into removing their original call for a plant-based diet, swapping it for a softer call to have a balanced diet or whatever bullshit, and that includes meat."

"You said a naughty word!" I try to sound amused, even though I'm terrified by what he's saying.

"It's not important. Don't tell Mum."

I shake my head.

"But what *is* important, is that the animal agriculture industry has too much power, and people are not ready to listen," Enav says.

"How come?"

"I don't know."

I feel like I'm about to cry. I'm afraid, and I'm confused. If there is a real way to change what's happening, why are people not doing it? What's more important than life on this planet? I don't get it.

Enav must see that I'm upset, so he decides to change the subject.

"Let's play 'can't touch the sand'," he suggests.

It's a game where we must only stand on the rocks. The first one to stumble and land on the soft sand, loses. I almost always lose.

The rocks here are old, and so smooth, they warm up by the sun, and feel nice to stand on. Enav hops and stands on one of the larger rocks, facing the sea, and starts singing in a deep, operatic voice; his arms waving to his sides, his face is expressive. He looks so funny, I must laugh.

"Don't laugh at the opera singer!" Enav says.

"You're no opera singer," I giggle.

"Not now, but one day I will be," Enav protests.

"How do you become an opera singer?" I ask.

"I don't know, you just sing. Maybe there's a university for opera singers or something."

"You sound silly," I giggle.

"I'll get better," he says with a smile. "Why? What do *you* want to be?"

"I'm going to be a mum!"

"A mum? That's your only ambition? You need to reach higher than that, Sis."

"What's wrong in wanting to be a mum?"

"You can be a mum and something more, like an astronaut, or a football referee, or a vegan pastry chef," Enav says.

"I'm going to have a daughter."

"Or a son, or both," Enav adds.

"No, a daughter. I already know who she is."

Enav looks at me, bemused. "Have you met her?"

I giggle. "Don't be silly! I'm only nine!"

I can't really tell him that in my heart, I've already met her. It's sort of weird, this feeling. It sometimes scares me, the connection that I already feel to someone who will be part of my life only in the future. I can't explain it, not even to myself. I just know it. I can feel it. It's like she's already part of me.

"Then how do you know who she is?"

"I know. I just know."

"Ok, so what's her name?"

"Tui."

"Tui? That's the name?"

"Yes, Tui."

"OK. It's nice."

"But Enav, what's going to happen to her, with the climate change I mean?"

Enav gives it a bit of thought.

"So, you already know that Tui's going to exist, do you?"

"Yes!"

"You should warn her, then," Enav says. "About climate change and all that."

"How can I warn her? She's not even born yet!" I giggle. Enav had some strange ideas.

"You can write her a letter!"

"A letter?"

"Yes, write her a letter, and give it to her when she's born." He thinks for a second, then continues, "No, actually, that won't do. You can give it to her when she can read!"

I laugh. "OK! Wait here, I'll get some papers and a pen. Don't go!"

I run back to the house, and rush inside like a storm.

"What's going on, Juni?" Mum asks.

"I need a paper and a pen, quick!"

"OK, OK. I'm sure I can find some for you," Mum says, as she opens some drawers and fishes out a few papers and a black pen. "Here you go."

"Thanks!" I grab them from her hands and run back to the beach. Enav is still there, still on the rocks, singing opera to the crabs.

"All good, Enav, I have it!" I say, panting from the running.

"Took you a while!" he says but doesn't seem upset.

"Sorry."

"Your friend was here," he says.

"What friend?" *I have no friends.*

"A boy. He came out of nowhere, nearly gave me a heart attack.

Asked for you."

"I don't know who you're talking about."

"He said he'll see you again some other time."

"But I don't know who you're talking about, Enav!" I say, frustrated. "I don't know any boys!"

"Maybe from school?"

"None of the boys is a friend of mine. What was his name?"

Enav scratches his head. "Erm... Uriah, I think."

"I don't know any Uriah."

Enav shrugs. I think he's just messing with me.

"OK, tell me what to write," I say. "On Tui's letter."

Suddenly Enav changes his body posture to look like some mad army general. His back stretched, his tummy poking forward, one arm folded across his chest. "I'm not Enav," he says, like some show-off, his head tilted up. "My name is Napoleon."

I giggle.

"So, you want my advice regarding this letter to your future child?"

"Yes, Enav," I laugh. "Sorry, I mean, yes, Napoleon."

"Very well, very well," Enav says, rolling the R's and sounding silly.

"Here we go. What's the name of this child, again?"

"Tui."

"Ah, very well. So, dear Tui—a warning."

"Wait!" I shout. "I need to sit down; I can't write like that." I drop onto the sand, the paper on my folded knees.

"OK, I'm ready now."

"For the last time child," Enav says, still in character. "Dear Tui—a warning." He dictates the letter in a dramatic tone. I try to catch up, writing what he says. I know it's important to write it word for word. One day, Tui will read it.

"I'm sorry that we—no, let me rephrase—I'm sorry—"

"Enav! You can't change the sentence in the middle! I've already written 'We no let me'!"

I'm getting frustrated.

"Try to keep up, Juniper, I'm Napoleon, and I'm a very busy man, I have lots more letters to dictate," he says, as he walks two steps to the left, then turns, and walks two steps back, repeatedly, like some pointless soldier.

"I'm sorry that the generations of my parents and their parents—"

"Slow down, Enav! You're too fast!"

"—have destroyed the planet for you. We didn't mean for this to happen. I'm sorry that your life will—"

I give up. I can't catch up to what he's saying. I'll take the letter home and try to remember what he says and write it up later.

"—be miserable. We gave people every opportunity to change.

We told them about the Plant Based Treaty, we told them about animal agriculture, but they are just like Napoleon, they don't care. Too selfish. Too greedy. So, there will be no future for you. Please take care, blah blah blah."

He's finished, looking very happy with himself.

"I didn't write it, because you were talking too fast!" I say, agitated.

Seeing my disappointment, Enav stops being Napoleon, and is himself again. "Nah, it wasn't important."

"But how will I warn her? I need to tell her about the planet, and the climate, and everything you said."

"It doesn't matter if you warn her or not, it's already happening anyway."

"But I need to write her the letter!"

"Then you can find your own words," Enav says.

Frustrated, I take Tui's letter and the pen and go back home.

I go straight to my room, put the letter on the desk and stare at it. I stare and stare, and I don't know what to write.

"Juniper, it's dinner time!" Mum calls me from the kitchen.

"Wait up, Mum, I'm doing something important!" I shout back. I keep staring at the letter.

Dear Tui,

A warning. I'm sorry that ~~we no let me that~~ the generations of my parents and their parents have destroyed the planet for you. We didn't mean for this to happen. I'm sorry that your life will—'

No, I don't want to write her all that. It's not what I want to say to her at all. What Enav said might be right, but I want to tell her something completely different.

I scratch it all, then restart the letter, a little below that paragraph:

'Dear Tui,

I already love you.

Mum.'

******

In **2018** a study was released in the journal **SCIENCE**. The study was a meta-data analysis that looked at **1530 studies** and analysed just under **40,000 farms** in **119 countries.** It looked at all different systems of farming (including grass-fed). It is the most comprehensive analysis to date of the impact that farming has on the environment.

The study showed that in high income nations, shifting to a plant-based diet would reduce agriculture emissions by **up to 73%**. Even the lowest-impact 'beef' is responsible for **6 times** more greenhouse gas emissions and **36 times** more land use than plant-based sources of protein. **83%** of all global agricultural land is used for animal farming, and yet it provides **less than 20%** of the calories and **less than 40%** of the protein that is consumed globally.

If the world shifted to a plant-based diet, we could feed everyone on the planet AND free up **more than 75%** of current agricultural land that could then be restored to help improve biodiversity. The land no longer required for food production could also be used to remove **8.1 BILLION** metric tonnes of CO2 from the atmosphere each year (which is about 15% of total annual emissions).

Lead researcher, Joseph Poore, stated: "A vegan diet is probably THE SINGLE BIGGEST WAY to reduce impact on Planet Earth, not just greenhouse gases, but global acidification, eutrophication, land use and water use".

Another research, published in SCIENCE in 2020, from the **University of Oxford**, stated that even if the use of fossil fuel was ended immediately, the emissions produced by the agricultural sector alone would make it **impossible to limit warming to 1.5 degrees Celsius** and would even make it difficult to not hit two degrees. This means changes to our food system are essential if we want to avoid a catastrophe. (Via: **SurgeActivism.org**)

TAKE ACTION

These are things you can do to ensure the future as depicted in this book, never comes true:

1. Go vegan (**veganeasy.org**)

2. Endorse the Plant Based Treaty (**plantbasedtreaty.org**)

3. Join city campaigns. Demand your local and national leaders to shift to a plant-based food system and economy (**plantbasedtreaty.org/campaign-hub**)

4. Get involved in climate activism: join or start a Plant Based Treaty team (**plantbasedtreaty.org/start-a-pbt-team**)

5. Support our ocean defenders (**paulwatsonfoundation.org**) *"If the ocean dies, we die."* *~Captain Paul Watson.*

More by M. C Ronen

'THE LIBERATION TRILOGY':

THE SHED

LIBERATION

IT WAS IN OUR HANDS

Praises for The Liberation Trilogy:

"As relevant to our generation as George Orwell's 1984 was to his. It should be required reading for everyone."
Louise Jane, VCA

Printed in Great Britain
by Amazon

28383952R00169